BASTION

Matthew Willis

First published in 2019 by Sharpe Books.

Table of Contents

BASTION

Week 1

16 June 1942

The city was shrieking, and Edmund Clydesdale was lost.

He stood, a ludicrous figure in Valletta's vertiginous streets. A little shorter than average, staring at the pale stone walls with wide-open eyes that were somewhere between grey and blue in colour. He might have been anything from 21 to 31, but the slightly-too-large Royal Navy Lieutenant's uniform he wore edged his appearance to the younger end. Even if the dark hollows and frown-lines around his eyes suggested the older.

An hour ago he'd been on a Royal Navy destroyer. A day ago, facing down waves of Stukas with a 20mm cannon. Two days ago, flying a Sea Hurricane in defence of a convoy, running out of fuel, bailing out over the sea... All to try and bring a few merchantmen to this island. Malta. Malta, the key to the Mediterranean. Malta, without which the Allies might not hold Egypt, the Suez Canal. Malta, the unsinkable aircraft carrier, the impenetrable submarine base. Malta, the most bombed place on Earth. And now he was standing on it. Lost.

Edmund had barely ascended the steps from the quay than he was swallowed by the city. His destination, the naval HQ at the Lascaris Bastion, was, he was told, no more than a quarter of a mile away, and easy to find, but as soon as he was among the tall stone buildings, all landmarks disappeared, and directions evaporated. Each street was like a canyon. Even then it should have been easy. Keep the water to the left and the hill to your right. He dodged round a knot of dockworkers heading down to the quay, then another swirled around him. The first turning was into a dug-up road, the second blocked by a stuck vehicle, and then an entire street that was nothing but heaps of rubble... He scuttled back the way he had come, turned up another street, implausibly steep, and before he realised it Edmund had no idea where he was. Legs burning, lungs heaving, eyes stinging.

He looked around for signs of where he might be. The street was all but empty. What had been shops were boarded up. What looked like a city from the outside was a ghost town within. Barely a pane of glass remained. Some of the buildings that looked complete were just hollow shells, one or two a facade standing and nothing behind it.

And that was when the air raid began.

The air trembled with sirens. They howled, echoing off walls and thundering up the streets. The fabric of Valletta vibrated with them. Then the AA burst out, booming in answer.

Edmund's borrowed kit bag slumped on the pavement. He'd just fought hundreds of German and Italian aircraft, crash landed in the sea and endured a naval battle on a destroyer. He glanced at the towering walls either side. For all he had been through, he didn't want to be killed by a fall of rubble. One bomb anywhere near this lot and you'd have no chance. A group of civilians came round the corner and walked past him. He opened his mouth to call them, but the shout ebbed away before it reached his mouth. He watched. They were moving as though the sirens had thickened the air. Edmund realised they were sauntering. Moving with purpose, but not urgency. Perhaps it was not so serious.

But there was another sound, sliding in between the bass of the guns and the treble of the sirens. A rising note, sharp and urgent.

Dive bombers.

The scream of speeding airscrews reverberated off the buildings. Impossible to tell which direction they were coming from. The crowd had thinned in the few moments his attention had been on the aircraft. Where had they gone? Just under cover? Or was there a shelter nearby? Some fragment of his brain cried that he should throw himself to the ground. He turned the idea over, examining from all sides. It did seem sensible. Then he felt the detonations through his feet, his lungs, and jumped six inches in the air from the suddenness of it. *Wait*, he thought. *I'm not ready*.

"What are you doing? Get to a shelter!"

Edmund whipped around at the shout. A lean form at the corner of the street. A woman. Maltese, he supposed. Holding herself upright, hands on hips. "Who are you?" he said, an instant later wondering why on Earth he'd asked that question of all the possible alternatives.

She hurried towards him, long strides, steady despite the juddering of the pavement. "You should go to a shelter, now." English spoken like a native, with the merest hint of a Mediterranean accent.

Edmund found himself staring slightly upwards into a pair of deep brown eyes. "I need to get to the Lascaris Bastion," he said, remembering himself. "I can't find the way."

The woman arched her eyebrows, and creases around her eyes hardened. "You need to get to the nearest shelter. Didn't you hear the sirens?"

The sirens were still howling, and both Edmund and the woman were shouting to make themselves heard.

"I have orders to report to Lascaris immediately," he said, trying to summon the authority of a naval lieutenant. The borrowed uniform suddenly felt awkward and he realised how hot he was.

The woman's stare hardened. "Follow me to a shelter. Or don't."

He tried to meet the glare, but a bomb went off a street or two away and his body betrayed him. "My orders..."

"They won't expect you to report in the middle of an air raid!"

"Look!" Edmund snapped, "I don't know who the hell you think you are but I need to get to Lascaris!"

The woman bristled. For a second Edmund thought she was going to spit on him or slap him. After a moment, she said "Do you have identification?"

"What? Yes." He patted his pocket.

"Good. At least we'll know who you are if you're killed." She pointed over his shoulder. "Cross there and take the next left, go all the way down to the end, where the street turns into steps. You'll see Grand Harbour ahead. Keep going in that direction, under an arch, until you can go no further. Lascaris will be on your right. Good luck Lieutenant. You'll need plenty."

Edmund's thanks died on his lips. The woman was already striding away. He hefted his kitbag and made to follow the directions. He'd barely got over the first crossroads when a roar of engines reverberated along the street. He had no idea which way the sound was coming from and turned his head wildly in all directions. The clatter of machine guns sent him diving to the ground. A vast shadow flickered over him, and another, smaller, while the bellow of engines reached a fortissimo. Edmund buried his head under the kitbag. Bombs. There would be bombs at any moment... But the engine roar lessened and he peeked upwards. A trail of smoke was dissipating in the slot of sky he could see, and that was all. Good God. He willed his arms and legs to help him up, but no more than a few paces on and another stick of bombs went off not far away and he hurled himself into a doorway, pulling his legs up, and covering his head with his arms. Why hadn't he gone to the shelter?

More aircraft screamed overhead, guns rattling, bullets pinging off the walls. He hunkered down harder. What the hell had been going through his head? Of course he should have gone to a shelter. What were they going to do, court martial him?

The anti-aircraft guns were louder now, more insistent. Probably the warships in the harbour had joined in with everything they had left after the convoy. He spared a fragment of thought for the crew of HMS *Hindscarth*, with whom he'd endured hours of air raids just like this one. Only it wasn't like this. Then, he was on a little ship, moving, hard to hit. More importantly he had a gun in his hands. Here, he was just cowering in a deserted, ruined city, waiting for a bomb to fall.

Could he make a run for it? No, safer here. Not if a bomb fell nearby, he wouldn't be. How far was it to the Bastion? He hadn't thought to ask. Jesus, why hadn't he followed that harpy who'd tried to bark orders at him?

The roar of the guns immersed him. The sound was physical, vibrating in his lungs, his head, up through the ground. He pressed his eyes tight shut, wrapped his arms over his head. He might have been there minutes or seconds. For long moments he could not disentangle whether he was cowering in a doorway in Valletta or standing at the cannon on HMS *Hindscarth*, blasting away at the swarming bombers. Just to get off this island. God, what a hellhole! Survive this, and he could go. Just hang on another few minutes and he'd be gone within a day or two. Maybe even by tonight. Just hang on.

There had been no more detonations nearby, or it seemed so. Perhaps the sound of the bombs had been trammelled up with the guns and he'd just not been able to distinguish them any more. He opened his eyes. In his ears was nothing but a high-pitched *eeeeee*, like a telephone dialling tone but higher, higher than a piccolo, almost out of hearing range. Had the guns stopped? And then another sound. Something like a voice, as though heard in a swimming pool, head underwater. A repetition. Three phrases. Then three more. Then the first three again.

It was sort of loudspeaker, nearby. A few moments more and Edmund heard "*Raiders passed, raiders passed, raiders passed,*" and then something impenetrable, a collision of syllables like "*Layranuplany-tal-adu-adu, layranuplany-tal-adu-adu, layranuplany-tal-adu-adu.*" Was it code? No, idiot. It must be Maltese.

Raiders passed. Did that mean all-clear? A moment later, the air-raid sirens wailed out again, this time holding a constant note. Yes. All-clear. Before he could stop himself, Edmund let out a sob, and tried to blink back tears but they'd already started and his face was wet and his eyes were stinging, burning. He couldn't see properly. The astringency of brick dust filled his nostrils, and his stomach heaved.

The all-clear sirens stopped. The loudspeakers stopped talking - and started playing music. Edmund started walking. The directions to Lascaris Bastion had all but ebbed out of his mind in their detail, but a general sense had remained like residue. He staggered under his kit bag in the rough direction the woman had pointed. After a while he found a street that became steps, an arch, and ahead the harbour. Seemingly more by luck than any conscious plan he found himself before a vast wall of stone, then declaring himself to a sentry and directed through a gate and into an antechamber. Within, another guard directed him to a clerk, and added "Oh, and by the way sir, there's a sink through there. Just in case you wanted to clean yourself up a bit."

Edmund caught a glimpse of himself in the glass of an office door. He was white with dust, his face especially, apart from two clean lines, running downward from his eyes. He stammered a thank you and proceeded to try to get rid of the worst of the muck and dirt. He then followed directions through the labyrinth to the officer commanding the island's naval air forces. By now he resented even the five minutes it took to get the filth off his face. It was potentially five more minutes he'd have to spend on Malta. Five more minutes until the leave he'd undoubtedly be owed in Gib. He'd had to bail out of his Hurri, went into the sea and then fought an AA gun on a destroyer against air raid after air raid. That should be worth a fortnight at least.

"Ah yes, Clydesdale," the Commander said when he'd been shown in. "Wasn't expecting you quite so soon, what with the air raid."

"No sir," he said stiffly. "I got caught out in it." *Can't you tell*?

The officer, Macleod, looked up at him sharply. "You mean you didn't get to a shelter? Didn't you hear the warnings?"

One could hardly miss them! "No sir. I mean, yes I did. But I couldn't... I mean, I didn't think it was far, and..."

Macleod frowned, harrumphed. "Yes, well. We get a lot of raids here and you won't last long if you don't get to shelter. It was only a handful of Savoia Marchettis going after the merchantmen, but you weren't to know it wasn't a bigger raid."

Just a handful of aircraft? And they weren't even all bombing the city? Edmund's mouth fell open and he slammed it shut again. Heavens. The noise. The blasts. It was as if the whole world was falling apart.

"...Next time listen to the warnings," Macleod went on. "There should be sirens and verbal notice through the Rediffusion system. That's the loudspeakers. You get radio programmes as well as public notices and... Well, someone will fill you in."

Edmund tried not to slump. "Aye sir, sorry sir." With any luck he should be off this rock by the end of the day anyway and shouldn't need to know too much about life in the hellhole. Tomorrow if not. Something Macleod had said a moment ago jumped to the front of Edmund's thoughts. "But. Erm, you said you were expecting me?"

"Yes, *Hindscarth* signalled."

Ah. Good, so they'd know of his ordeal. He would be back to Gib in a matter of hours.

"...So. Now we have to work out what to do with you."

Edmund shifted awkwardly. He'd started to feel increasingly stiff in his limbs. *What to do with him*? Wasn't that obvious? "I'd hoped to rejoin my squadron as soon as possible, sir. My ship. If there's going to be another convoy soon..." And leave. A week or two's leave. Three would be nice.

Macleod had started looking over a typewritten sheaf of papers and did not look up. "Without wishing to give too much away, there won't be another effort like Operation 'Harpoon' for over a month, two perhaps, though there might be a run to transfer some more Spitfires in a while. We're going to have to hang on here a little longer."

That was a pity for the island, but no concern of Edmund's. Not at this moment. "Oh. I see sir. So when might I expect to be returned to *Eagle*?"

"Well. At some point we might be able put you on a Hudson to North Front and you can rejoin your squadron from there."

At some point?

"...But space and fuel are at a premium, and in any case it would be more useful to have you here for a couple of weeks. Three, perhaps."

Here? On Malta? Weeks! Edmund felt as though his stomach was full of that ghastly brick dust. It wasn't possible. Had he just sailed through hell for this? Hateful tears started pricking at his eyes again. "Here, sir?" he said as levelly as he could manage. "You mean stay on Malta? What would I do?" Perhaps there was some misunderstanding. Perhaps he did not mean *here*, here.

Macleod raised an eyebrow. "Yes, here. We have a few Hurricanes attached to the Naval Air Squadron at Hal Far. The OC's got Albacore pilots flying them at the moment, but it would be handy if you could take one over for a bit. Given that it's your type."

Flying here? On Malta...? He'd heard the stories. Weaving on take-off to dodge the craters and falling bombs, and if you managed to get into the air and one of the thousands of fighters from Sicily didn't get you, you'd just as easily come a cropper on landing on the pitted, wreck-strewn airfields. Oh yes, he'd heard the stories alright. "Aye, sir," he replied, trying not to stammer. "But Hurris? I thought it was all Spits for air defence here these days?"

"Only since last month. Oh, but no, it wouldn't be for air defence. We use the Hurris for ASR."

Air-sea rescue? Edmund stared. Not combat? But it was a very particular kind of flying. Had the Commander mixed him up with someone else? "I'm afraid I don't have any training in ASR sir."

Macleod held Edmund's gaze and exhaled through his nose. "Nobody has training for anything specialised out here, you just have to pick it up. The pilots I've got on it at the moment aren't ASR trained. They're not even fully trained on type. We've had ASR flights shot down because the pilots were too busy searching for dinghies and didn't see the fighters that got them. It's rare, thank heaven. But that's where your experience should come in handy."

"I see sir. But my squadron-"

"Doesn't need you immediately. We do."

Macleod had carried out this conversation with pilots before, Edmund realised. Perhaps many times. Much as though he wanted to get out of here as soon as possible, Edmund did not want to make life difficult for those who didn't have the chance. He nodded slowly. "I see sir." Three weeks. But at least it would not be air defence. Perhaps it wouldn't be so bad. Even a rest, of sorts. And as for his squadron not needing him...they were probably happy to be rid of him.

Macleod affected to look kindly. The Commander must have seen the misgivings written on his face, and leapt to the wrong conclusion. "Look, if it's the ASR you're concerned about, that it's not strictly a combat role... A lot of pilots end up in the drink. We need every single one we can pull back out. I could lend you to the RAF, they'd put you in a Spit, and you'd be one pilot. And you'd be gone in a few weeks. This way, over the same time you might save half a dozen others who can all get back into the fight."

Edmund was about to reply when Macleod twisted his mouth and said "And, er... Occasionally the ASR flights run into enemy aircraft, so it helps that you're actually a fighter pilot."

Edmund wondered how 'occasionally'. He said nothing.

"...And it frees up one torpedo bomber pilot for shipping strikes of course," Macleod quickly added. "Assuming we can get the petrol for that. But look. If you really want to go to a fighter squadron while you're here, that can certainly be arranged. Maybe get that fifth kill, eh?"

Edmund's eyes widened and it was all he could do to stop himself barking *no!* at the Commander. He affected to smile, but it felt more like a grimace across his face. "Thank you, sir. I think the ASR sounds like the best idea, and I'd hate to put you to any trouble."

A flicker of disappointment passed over Macleod's face, then something like relief and he dismissed Edmund with an order to get to Hal Far as soon as he could.

***

After Edmund wandered out of the office and collected a few chits for various things from the Commander's secretary, he promptly got lost again. He went through a door and found himself in an enormous control room, map table, WAAFs with croupier rakes, and a collection of personnel from all three services, all of whom were staring at him. He turned tail and eventually found his way back to the security officer looking after his kitbag. Yet another set of garbled directions and he was back in the Mediterranean sun.

There was no transport to Hal Far. Just a half-wrecked bus. It had no glass in its windows and a hot, dusty draught blasted Edmund as the vehicle jolted and crashed its way to his new temporary home. The landscape the bus weaved its way through was an unsettling clash of the familiar and the alien. Little green and virtually no trees, the arid vista was the colour of hay, rock and sun-baked dirt, yet the wandering lanes and dry-stone walls could have been transplanted from the Yorkshire Dales or Cumberland. It was what England might look like in a million years under the aged sun, swollen and lurid. Edmund shuddered. Three weeks... He settled down into his misery. His shipmates and such friends as he could lay claim to were half the Mediterranean away in Gib, by now. His girlfriend – could he even call her that? – the half-hearted Wren, was half a continent away, in Scotland. And yet he felt no more alone now than he had before the squadron left Turnhouse to come south.

After the best part of an hour, an aircraft, gear down, roared overhead and Edmund craned his neck to see where it had come from. The fenced-off expanse to the right could be nothing but an airfield. But no, this was Luqa, according to an RAF airman whose stop this was. Hal Far – Edmund still wasn't sure whether it was technically a Royal Navy or RAF air station, or whether such things mattered on Malta – was at least as far again. It was nowhere in sight by the time the bus skirted a low hill and juddered to a stop, the driver shouting in fragments Maltese and English that the remaining passengers should get out here. The road was tumbled across with debris, evidently from bomb hits somewhere up the slope. A party of soldiers had only just started shovelling the dirt and rubble clear away.

The five civilians Edmund shared the vehicle with disembarked with no sign of surprise and headed away with apparent purpose. Edmund asked the driver for directions. The driver looked at him with suspicion, as if an Axis spy would wear a British naval uniform and have quite such little sense of where he was. He received yet more directions – these were simple enough, follow the road and at its end he would reach the airfield – and set out. The sun was like the mouth of a furnace. His clothes turned to sandpaper. He began to gain another coating of dust. Eventually, he crested a brow and there were buildings ahead, low, bleached-white pre-war messes and barrack-blocks. And hangars, thank Christ. Just beyond was the ink-line of the sea.

It took an age to trudge to the main gate. He handed his papers to a guard, a soldier accompanied him to the officer commanding, Lieutenant-Commander Haynes. "An Australian," his escort explained, profoundly. Edmund affected to look knowing. He had never met any Australians.

Haynes was expecting him. If one thing worked on this rotten island, it was the communications. "Good to have you with us," the officer grinned as soon as Edmund had walked through into the office and saluted. Haynes returned the salute and pushed his cap back on his head. Together with his pointed beard the gesture made Haynes look more like a submarine commander than a torpedo squadron CO. "I can't tell you. I've been flying ASR myself so you being here takes the pressure off me no end. I'll introduce you to the other musketeers." He shouted to his secretary to *go get Subs Godden and Cocke wouldya*?, and turned back to Edmund.

"S'pose I should introduce myself properly. I'm Haynes, CO of 828 Squadron. It's a bit complicated. We're arranged as a single unit here for the minute, called the Naval Air Squadron, but us and 830 are still nominally commissioned and all that. Eight-Thirty acts as a flight. They're on Stringbags, we've got Albacores, but they've only got three machines left."

"I see, sir," Edmund said, not at all sure that he did. "Captain Macleod mentioned some Hurricanes?"

"Yep, and that's where you come in. I've transferred two Subs from Applecores, we don't have the kites for them anyway. Where the hell are those two? Kiwis, but you have to work with what you've got, *haha*! Don't know how much Macleod told you, but we got landed with ASR protection about a month ago. The launches are RAF, and they mostly fish RAF bods out of the drink so naturally someone decided escorting them was Navy business. Don't ask me why. Where the hell have those Subs got to? We got a few Hurris transferred from RAF stocks, one for spares, the rest to fly until they wear out. The procedure is simply this. If the launch is called out to a downed aircraft and there are any enemy pilots on the board, they call us and we scramble a Hurri or two. We have two jobs – keep an eye out for fighters and help the boat search. We can see more than they can, so we can help minimise their time exposed. Both help in case someone decides to shoot them up. The boat or the ditched crews."

What on Earth? Edmund whistled. Shooting at unarmed men in dinghies? At rescue services? "Good Lord! Do they do that? Captain Macleod mentioned that you run into fighters from time to time, but he didn't say anything about the launches getting strafed!"

"Very occasionally. Now and then. The Eyeties leave us alone, but the Germans were a little more difficult. There've been protests made, of course. They claim that we're lying, that their pilots mistook our rescue launches for MTBs, or that we're up to no good and the boats were a legitimate target. More often when we run into fighters they're out looking for their own ditched crews and don't bother us. Fortunately, we're only facing Eyeties at the moment. Jerry's recently buggered off to bother Joe Stalin. Truth is, it's mainly a deterrent. If the Eyeties know there's a fighter up, they think twice about interfering with the launch."

A deterrent. Well that didn't sound too bad.

"...Anyway, spot the pilots in the drink and direct the launches to pick them up," the squadron commander went on. "Keep an eye out for bandits. You need good eyesight, a bit of a sixth sense maybe. But that's the job. Ah, here they are."

Haynes had reacted to the sound of the outer office door being opened, and a moment later there was a knock at the door, which opened, and the secretary's head appeared.

"I could only find Mr Godden sir, shall I keep looking for Mr Cocke?"

Haynes rolled his eyes. "Never mind. Show Godden in."

A stocky, stubbly figure entered, threw the sloppiest salute Edmund had seen in years at Haynes, and toppled into a chair. He was dressed in a pair of RAF khaki drill shorts and a threadbare naval jacket.

"No need to stand on ceremony," Haynes muttered.

"Thank you, sir," the newcomer said, in an antipodean drawl. He nodded at Edmund. "So, who's this?"

Haynes went on as if the other officer had not just committed half a dozen disciplinary offences in a matter of seconds. "Clydesdale, this is Sub-Lieutenant Godden. He'll be ASR Flight Leader, don't mind being under the command of a junior officer do you? Good, good. Godden, this is Lieutenant Clydesdale. We've borrowed him from HMS *Eagle*. He'll be joining you on the Hurri flight for the next few weeks."

"Good-oh."

"Show him the ropes, would you? Couple of days familiarisation. He can shadow a call-out if we get any. And then in at the deep end."

"Wilco, Skip."

Under a junior officer? Only a couple of days' familiarisation? Edmund's throat seemed to have closed-up. He tried to take a breath. It didn't seem enough. He thought about saying something but couldn't imagine what it would be.

"...And track down Cocke and fill him in, he'll need to know what's what too." Haynes turned back to Edmund. "Well, that's all for now. Godden'll show you to your cabin. No, don't worry about your kit, a steward'll bring it over. Oh. And one last thing. Do you have any special skills we might be able to call on while you're here?"

Edmund blinked. What did he mean? "I speak French rather well. I, er, know a lot of French poetry, it was...ah...at university."

Haynes' eyes bulged. Edmund realised he was trying desperately not to laugh. "I meant more in terms of practicalities. We used to have a chap who'd worked for General Electric – fixed all the lights and built a heater for the winter. Never mind, though. If ever there's a call for French poetry, you'll be the first to know."

Edmund left the office feeling as though his face was on fire and as soon as the outer door had closed behind them, Godden exploded in laughter. "French poetry eh? Whatever next. Still, perhaps you could infiltrate the Vichy Frogs in North Africa pretending to be a wandering bard or something. Do you play the lute as well? Marvellous!" He looked at Edmund. "What's the matter?" And bellowed with laughter once again.

Godden escorted Edmund around the air station in the same lax and downright insolent manner he'd displayed from his first appearance. Discipline here must be as bad as everything else.

He thought of the civilian woman in Valletta barking orders like a drill sergeant and the Lieutenant Commander he'd just met letting a junior officer act as though he owned the place. It was upside down and inside out.

Edmund saw the wardroom, the bomb shelters, his 'cabin' – a cubicle in a cinderblock shed – and headed out onto the heat of the airfield. It seemed little but a sunburned expanse. Although technically one could take off in any direction, a pale worn-smooth strip bisecting the field revealed that the wind must be almost always in the same direction. Edmund counted three army parties around the site, filling in holes. The entire airfield was riddled with everything from what the pongoes termed '*holes, pot, small*' to '*craters, bomb, bloody enormous*.'

Glowering around the edges were the shattered and burned out wrecks of a dozen aircraft. Hard to tell what they'd been before they became sun-scorched, twisted wreckage. A Blenheim or two, some Spits, a Hurri, a biplane that might have been anything. Here and there, incandescent points like miniature stars blazed back the sun where it had found an edge of bright, bare metal. It hurt to look at them.

At least the dispersal pens looked neat and tidy, the revetments built up with almost mathematical neatness. When they had got a bit closer, he exclaimed "Good Lord, are those made out of fuel cans?"

"Absolutely," Godden replied. "Don't worry, no fuel in them now. Filled with dirt, they make decent blast shelters for the kites."

Edmund shook his head in wonder. "But how on Earth have you so many of the things going spare?" They were still a few paces away and he could feel the heat radiating off the baked metal.

"That's what we get our fuel delivered in," Godden said, suddenly serious. "Haven't had a tanker through in over a year.

Instead all they can manage to send is submarines and the odd fast minelayer, loaded to the gunwales with small cans. Got no use for the containers once the fuel's in bowsers, so-" he kicked the wall of metal, which thudded, "might as well. Anyway, I'll show you our Hurris."

***

Edmund had consoled himself that however out of his depth he felt, he would at least be reasonably safe, given that his role was not strictly a combat one. On seeing the Hurricanes he would be flying, he revised that opinion drastically.

"Here we are!" said Godden, with quite unwarranted pride, waving two seaman's-cap wearing erks to one side. "The last three operational Hurricanes on the island. *Faithless*, *Hopeless* and *Uncharitable*."

Edmund's laugh died in his throat. The three aircraft were wrecks. Back home they surely would have been on the scrapheap long before now. They were Mark Two Hurricanes, the B model with twelve guns, though these had had the outer four removed and faired over. That should help the performance a little bit. Even though they were ostensibly newer than Edmund's Mark One Sea Hurricane back on *Eagle*, he'd swap that for these machines any day of the week. *Faithless*, *Hopeless* and *Uncharitable* had been repainted in a dark blue-grey, but patches had worn and flaked off, especially on the wings, which gave a blotched appearance. Behind the exhaust, the fuselage was coated with thick, black stains curving down over the wing and discolouring the surface as far back as the cockpit. The engines evidently weren't running too cleanly... Underneath, the paint was streaked with dirty trails where oil and lubricant had leaked and found its way out though the cowling panels, smeared by the airflow. They must have been fighter-bombers in their previous life – the erks hadn't even taken the bomb carriers off.

"You fly these?" Edmund asked. "On purpose?" Immediately he bit his lip. The erks were still standing there, and the last thing he wanted to do was offend them.

Godden laughed. "When you've been lumbering about in an Albacore, even a knackered Hurricane is a delight."

"The maintainers must be miracle workers."

"Oh, they are, they are! Hey Mike, I took *Hopeless* up this morning, the engine's running sweet as a nut," Godden called to one of the erks, who were fiddling about towards the tail. The named maintainer smiled tightly and went back to his work.

"As a matter of fact-" Godden lowered his voice and leaned in. "I've got something brewing and these kites will be just the ticket for it. Can't really tell you about it here, but...hang about, there he is."

Godden pointed. Edmund followed his outstretched arm. There was no-one in sight. He squinted. Hundreds of yards away, rippled with heat-haze, a figure sat next to a revetment. Edmund would never have spotted him. "Sub-Lieutenant Cocke," Godden added. "See?"

How on Earth could he tell that from here? Must have eyes like a hawk. "I think I can see why Commander Haynes gave you the ASR role," Edmund breathed.

"Oh, that? He caught me trying some aerobatics in an Albacore and figured I'd be less of a risk in a Hurricane."

Edmund blinked. "Aerobatics? An Albacore?"

"It was just a barrel roll. Positive G all the way. Don't see what the problem was."

Aerobatics? An Albacore? Edmund shook his head. "I can't imagine."

"If I'd done it without a torpedo, no-one would have batted an eyelid."

"A live torpedo?" Edmund's mouth opened and closed like that of a fish. He could feel it happening but could apparently do nothing to stop it.

Godden nodded, as if this was normal. "Anyway, let's go and catch Cocke before he drifts off somewhere else."

The figure they were approaching was seated on an old ammunition crate, and apparently writing in a large white book which he would stare at intently for a few moments, then glance up at something across the airfield.

"Cocke's our liaison to the marine unit down at Kalafrana," Godden said as they walked. "He'll take you down and introduce you to them. Oh, wait a sec." He put his hand on Edmund's arm. "Listen."

Edmund did as he was told. For a moment, nothing, just the breeze gusting gently across the flat land, rushing softly around the revetments. And then he heard it. The hum of engines. He tensed, ready to run for the nearest shelter, but Godden said "look, it's the recce kite!" and pointed just above the horizon. Edmund could see nothing, but the sound of engines swelled, and in a few moments he caught it, a thin line with three blobs near the middle, which resolved into a Martin Baltimore, yowling right overhead and along the runway before pulling into a turn and joining the circuit. "Gotta go, they're back from Sicily," Godden panted, as if that explained anything. He formed a trumpet with his hands and bellowed "hey, Cocke! Where the hell have you been? Haynes is hopping mad!"

Cocke looked up. Edmund was close enough that he could make out surprise, annoyance and confusion on his face in that order.

"Got the new boy here," Godden went on, "he's a French poet! Show him the ropes won't you!" and he turned tail and ran.

"Hallo," Edmund said, after a moment marvelling at Godden's extraordinary behaviour. "Do I have the pleasure of addressing the squadron's liaison to the ASR unit?"

Cocke glanced at Edmund's stripe, clambered to his feet and saluted. "Sir," he nodded.

At least discipline here wasn't completely shot, then. Edmund returned the salute. "Clydesdale. Don't worry about the sir. People call me Clyde, mostly."

Cocke nodded. "Sub Le'tenant Cocke. Pronounced 'Coke', though plenty of fellows find it amusing to pronounce it 'cock'. They think it's original, I suppose."

Edmund hadn't realised it was spelled that way. He shrugged. "Ah. Yes."

"You can call me Viv if you prefer," Cocke added. "But, you're not French?"

Edmund snorted. "I think that was just Godden's idea of a joke."

"Oh." Cocke looked disappointed. Edmund seemed to be destined to disappoint people today. He took a proper look at Cocke for the first time. He was tall and rather spare – though everyone round here looked rather spare, now Edmund thought about it. His eyes were the kind of blue that in a cheap novel might be called 'striking', and his face, narrow and all sharp corners, also fell into that category. Though the effect was somewhat offset by uneven clumps of hair attached to his jaw and across his upper lip, coloured blond or brown seemingly at random. Edmund realised Cocke had noticed him staring at the unfortunate facial hair.

"Er, does every naval officer round here have a beard?" He smiled, feeling the awkward tightness of it. "Everyone I've met so far seems to. Seems positively Elizabethan."

Cocke smiled back just as self-consciously. "Razor blades are in short supply on the island. Like most things. Regs say the

RAF chaps need to be clean shaven. We don't, so most of us exchanged any blades we had with them for something more useful." He tugged at one of the thicker patches on his cheek. "Mine's taking a while to come through properly."

To Edmund's surprise he liked Cocke instantly. Cocke offered him a cigarette – Edmund shook his head – and set about lighting one for himself as though it were something that required total concentration, each small operation carried out deliberately and slowly. It was a ritual that had something almost religious about it. The cigarette finally lit. It smelled foul.

"You didn't bring any cigarettes, did you?" Cocke said to him after he'd taken his first puff. Edmund shook his head. "Shame," Cocke went on. "You would have been a rich man." He sighed expansively. "It would be splendid to smoke something other than these blasted Cape to Cairo things. Even once in a while. I don't half miss Players."

"I can imagine." For a moment they regarded each other. Edmund tried to remember why he was here. "Well. Anyway. I'm here for a few weeks. Joining you on this ASR business."

Cocke frowned and sighed. "Only a few weeks? That's a pity. Hoped your arrival meant I could get back to anti-shipping."

"Sorry. I'm only here because I was shot down during the convoy."

At that, Cocke seemed interested for the first time. "Shot down? Blimey. But you're alright? What was it like?"

"Yes, I suppose I am. Alright, I mean. It all happened rather quickly I'm afraid." *A hurricane blasting past him...battering...an explosion of black cold, white stars...* Edmund suppressed a shudder. "I wouldn't entirely recommend it."

They chatted for a while about ASR flying. Procedures, working with the rescue launch. The chances of running into the enemy. Cocke made it sound straightforward, and Edmund felt a little more sure of things.

Just then, the wind blew up, and Edmund and Cocke clapped their hands onto their hats. Cocke's book flipped open, the pages snapping in the gust, and fell to rest spread like a bird's wings. Edmund could not stop himself peering at it. The paper was covered not with writing but with dark lines and blocks. "You were drawing!" he said, instantly wishing he'd kept the thought in his head.

Cocke's face turned pinker. "Just a bit of sketching to pass the time," he muttered.

Edmund thought it must be a bit more than that. The sketch on the open page – it looked like the main mess building during an air raid – spoke of seriousness, of attention to the craft, of a singular energy. "Might I have a look?" he asked.

Cocke coloured even more deeply, but handed the sketchbook over. Edmund flipped through a few pages. They were all scenes of Malta, and all involving some kind of action. An air raid. Re-arming a Spitfire. Going into an air raid shelter. "These are alright," he said, again wincing at his choice of words. "I mean, you're good." He flipped the book shut and handed it back. "Artist before the war?"

"Not really. A student." Cocke avoided his gaze, lighting another cigarette. He seemed to be having some difficulty holding the match steady, though that might just have been the wind. "Didn't properly start 'til I got out here. I paint, really. These are just ideas and something to paint from. It's not very practical to lug an easel and a whole box of oil paints around the airfield. Especially not with all the alerts."

They stood again for a moment, Edmund wondering what to say. Before he could think of something, Cocke said "Is the poetry you write in French then? If you're not? French, I mean."

"Oh!" Why on Earth had he mentioned that? What an idiot. "No, I don't write poetry. Godden must've got the wrong end of the stick. I study it. Or I did. Still read a lot. French poetry."

"Ah." Cocke met his gaze. "Why?"

"Why what?"

"Why not write?"

Edmund raised an eyebrow, took his cap off and scratched his head. Why not? "Well. I'm not a poet."

"You understand poetry. You must have some affinity with it. Love for it, even."

Edmund felt himself buckling under the icy blue gaze. Itchy. "I don't know...it didn't occur to me. There's a war on."

Cocke shrugged. "I think that makes it more important than ever. Don't you? To find a language. Some way to express all this?"

***

By the time Edmund finally got a moment to himself, retreating to the room he'd been allocated, he was physically exhausted – it was early afternoon and he'd been rushing around since five in the morning, after a couple of hours fitful doze on HMS *Hindscarth* as they were making their way into the harbour. All he'd eaten since he left the destroyer was a slice of bread with a cup of tea doled out at the mess. Three cups of tea a day. That was all anyone was allowed here. Three! If he moved too quickly, everything started to spin.

His mind, though, was vibrating with energy. He dug out some writing paper and a pencil. Edmund stared at the blank sheet for the best part of a minute, everything that had happened to him in the last few days flickering behind his eyes. And then, instead of poetry, he started to write a letter to the journalist, Vickery, who he'd shared a cabin with on HMS *Eagle*. It felt as though it had been weeks ago, but was only three days. He had no idea if the letter would reach Vickery – indeed, very little idea where he might address it – but it felt good to be doing something, and cathartic to pour everything that had befallen him since he last spoke to the reporter. Running out of fuel during a dogfight, bailing out, being scooped up by a destroyer and then the sea battle with the Italian cruisers... Even so, recently it had begun to feel like something that happened to someone else, or in another lifetime.

That done, he lay on his bed and closed his eyes. A moment later, the door banged open and Godden strode in. "Grab your kit, we're going for a joyride."

Edmund sat up, rubbed his face. "A what?"

"Chop chop. The boat's had a call-out, there are no bogeys on the grid, so off we go." He marched out, calling back down the corridor, "Perfect opportunity to get your eye in."

Edmund lunged for his flying helmet, his goggles, pulled his salt-stained shoes on and ran after Godden.

"What's the flight plan?" he puffed when he'd caught up with the other pilot. "Where are we going?"

"Just stay on me. Worry about details when you're operational." He turned to Edmund and grinned. "Stop fretting so much, this is the time to have a bit of fun."

Edmund wasn't sure he had the same idea of fun as someone who would barrel roll a three-man biplane with a sixteen-hundred pound torpedo slung beneath it, but said nothing. Godden showed him to his Hurricane – *Hopeless* – introduced him to his rigger, fitter and armourer, and jogged off to his own machine. As soon as Edmund finished his walk-round of the machine and settled down into the cockpit, the smell of oil, leather, hot metal flooding his nostrils, sheer familiarity began to calm his nerves. He recognised the erk Godden had spoken to before, Mike, as his fitter. "I've just come off Mark Ones," he said as he familiarised himself with the controls. "Remind me when I need to switch supercharger gear?"

Mike smiled warmly, evidently happy to be asked. "If you're climbing on plus twelve boost, change to full when static boost has dropped about five PSI." They discussed a few other details, wireless frequencies, economic climbing speeds and so on, while Joe, the rigger, leaned in and tightened his harness straps.

Edmund noticed that the Hurricane was wired for bomb release. "Any chance when I get back that we could take the bomb racks off her?" he asked Mike. "It'd make a bit of difference to performance. Fuel consumption too."

Mike twisted his mouth awkwardly. "Sorry sir, Mr Godden wants them left on. I think we might be getting drop tanks and dinghy packs."

Well, then put the racks back on if those items arrive? Edmund shrugged and pushed the thought to the back of his mind. Then they started the engine and Edmund went through his last checks. He'd barely finished when Godden taxied past in a blast of dusty propwash. Edmund had to rush to keep up, pushing the cold engine harder than he'd like. He realised Godden was taxiing cross-wind, and rather close to one of the parties of pongoes filling craters. He fiddled with the wireless switch but just before he ran into the soldiers, Godden noticed and swerved away, almost ground-looping in the attempt, one main gear wheel hopping off the ground. By the time they'd lined up at the end of the runway, Edmund's heart was beating a tattoo. He heard the roar as Godden opened his throttle. For a moment Edmund thought it was a last full power engine check, but Godden was rolling, and Edmund pushed his throttle to the gate too. In a moment, the two Hurricanes were bouncing, dancing, in the in-between state between groundbound and flying, and finally airborne.

Once he had a few hundred feet of air under his wings and the undercarriage was safely tucked away, Edmund tipped the Hurricane's wings and took a good look at the land below. The fields were crossed and recrossed by walls which curved and looped like unintelligible handwriting in a lost language. There was nowhere to put down. Nowhere. The road would be best, but even that was impossible, too narrow, too twisting. An engine failure was death. Fuel starvation was death. A dead-stick meant a dead pilot. Edmund fought to breathe.

But Godden was making a wide climbing turn to the left. Thanks be to Jesus, he seemed a bit more steady in the air than on the ground. Edmund slotted in on the outside, and after a few more minutes the sea lay ahead, dark and endless as night. The radio clicked in his ears and Godden's voice cut in. "Hello Gondar, this is Exile Flight. We are airborne angels two, steering zero-eight-zero, please give vector for Seagull."

Exile flight? That was the call sign? How apt.

"Hello Exile Leader," the controller's voice rasped out of the headphones. At first Edmund thought the signal strength must be poor. Then he realised the controller really did sound that gruff. "Steer zero three two."

The two Hurricanes swung to the northward, suspended in blue. "Keep your eyes peeled," Godden said to him, "and let me know when you see the launch. I'll be arse-end charlie."

"Wilco." Edmund studied the indigo plain ahead. It ought to be possible to see anything down there, but a further glance revealed faint haze sitting above the water, smearing everything with grey.

The sea appeared completely empty. Edmund was aware of Sicily, looming in his consciousness in the haze beyond the horizon – barely beyond – left of the nose. He scanned left to right, devoting as much attention to that as he could spare, the minimum to the instruments, maintaining course, speed, altitude, monitoring engine temps, oil pressure, the myriad things that could kill you if they edged out of the narrow window. To the left, to the right, back to the left. Steady, constant...how far out was that launch anyway?

Ah, there. Right up where the horizon smudged into the grey. The tiniest white mark. Checked again. The V of a wake. At that distance it was definitely a small craft. He called it in to Godden, pleased with how quickly he'd seen it.

"About bloody time," Godden laughed. "I had it nearly a minute. Not bad for first time I suppose. Alright, switching frequency, let's see if we can talk to them." Edmund fiddled with the VHF, and soon heard "Seagull Zero-Seven, this is Exile Leader, I see you and will be overhead shortly."

"Good to hear you, Exile Flight," hissed back over the airwaves. "Fighters patrolling towards Sicily reported a dinghy. Could be from a bomber or night fighter shot down or ditched last night. There was a bit of argy bargy over the Alexandria convoy that turned back." The Wireless Op read out a position, perhaps 25 miles from the Sicilian coast.

"Understood," Godden said. "We'll keep an eye out. Hello Exile Two, I'll take the lead now. You keep them skinned for fighters."

"Yes, Exile Leader." Well, that was something he was more familiar with at least, but Edmund was still stinging over Godden's comment about how long he'd taken to spot the launch. They flew over the boat, waggling their wings, and began an orbit a couple of miles ahead of it. Forty minutes later, Godden called the launch. He'd seen the dinghy, but it didn't look as though there was anyone in it. The launch caught up and confirmed the finding. Edmund could hear the Wireless Operator's desolation. He felt more deflated than he imagined he could. After all, the chances of finding something so small as a person in a huge stretch of sea like this must be tiny. And yet it was their sole purpose. Each life was vital to Malta's struggle. They kept searching for as long as the fuel allowed, finding nothing. No bodies, alive or otherwise. And then Godden called bingo, and they turned for Malta, seeming to trudge through the sky as they left the launch, tiny and pitching, behind in the immensity.

Perhaps to try and raise spirits, Godden took them down to low level as they approached the coast. “Follow the leader,” he radioed, and dropped his Hurricane until it was hugging the terrain, jinking around hills, darting through valleys, a wake of dust blooming in his propwash. Edmund’s heart was thundering in his ears. His palms were slick on the spade grip. “Lower,” Godden called. Edmund was already as low as he dared – well under fifty feet, but he swallowed hard and shaved a few feet off. Every time he banked it felt as though the wingtip would crunch into the ground and then it would all be over. Godden snicked this way and that, then straightened out, and Edmund realised they were racing along a road, climbing a slope towards a brow. In the next instant, Godden’s Hurricane whisked upwards as if it had been tweaked by a giant puppeteer. Edmund pulled up, sensing something red and yellow looming in his path, and his Hurricane skimmed over a bus that had just crested the rise. For a moment Edmund could hear nothing but his own breathing, hard in the oxygen mask, but then he became aware of Godden’s laughter through his headphones.

“Your first ASR flight,” Godden said to him after they were down and safe. His heart was still cantering in his ribcage. “How was it?”

“Depressing,” Edmund replied. “All that and no-one there. Just a dinghy.”

It was possible the dinghy had just broken free from a crashed aircraft as it sank. It was equally possible that there had been someone in it until, delirious or unconscious, they had fallen out and drowned.

Godden shrugged. “Truth is, most calls are like that. In fact, with most calls, there isn’t even a dinghy. Worst, we do rescue someone and it’s an Eyetie or a bloody Jerry. No.” He paused for a while, evidently weighing his words. Then seemed to snap back to the moment, smiled, a little wanly and said “I propose I take you to The Gut. After all, you only live once.”

“What on Earth is The Gut?” It did not sound in the least appealing. Edmund looked at Godden, sidelong, to see if this was another joke he didn’t understand.

Godden clapped him on the shoulder and smirked, showing a predatory tooth. “You’ll find out, Clyde old son, and then you’ll wonder how you ever lived without it.”

Edmund sighed. “Honestly, I just need sleep. I’ve been up since the crack of doom and barely slept a wink on the destroyer. I appreciate it, but I don’t think I can manage a night on the town.”

Godden shook his head. “Hmm. I suppose. Explains why you couldn’t see a damned thing out there ‘til it was in front of your face, I guess. All right, well we can do another familiarisation flight tomorrow afternoon, or if we get a call out you can tag along. Go with Cocke to Kalafrana to see the boat in the morning. Then in the evening we paint the town red. Alright? After that you’re a fully- fledged member of the flight, and no room for slacking. I’ve plans for you, my lad, big plans.” He clapped Edmund on the shoulder again, and strode away, calling back over his shoulder “Big plans!”

Edmund shook his head and retreated to his room. He fell onto the bed without taking so much as a shoe off, and within a moment was submerged in sleep. He did not wake until a shriek and a concussion from outside brought him to his feet. Without quiet knowing how, he found himself standing, half dressed, in cool night air outside the barrack block, alone. There were sirens blaring, but they sounded a long way off. The crump-

crump of bombs and AA was barely audible. In the room it had been deafening, somehow.

Something hissed nearby in the darkness and a light glared briefly a few yards away. Edmund whipped around but could only see the orange glow of a lit cigarette.

"It's alright," a voice drifted out of the gloom. "Which is to say it's alright for us. Valletta's getting it."

"Cocke?"

"Mm-hmm." Cocke took a long drag on the cigarette, and the tip glowed brighter. "You get used to it. Don't you worry, if there's an alert here, you'll know all about it."

Edmund scanned the skyline. There was a glow on the horizon to the North West. Searchlight beams swung and toppled lazily, like giraffe necks made of light.

"Full moon. Makes the harbour easy to see from the air," Cocke added.

"It woke you up."

"No. I was awake anyway. Nobody here sleeps too well. Except Godden, perhaps."

Edmund yawned. "I wish I knew his secret. I should go back to bed. I've a feeling tomorrow's going to be another long day."

"They all are, old man," Cocke murmured.

***

The following morning, Edmund found his way back to the mess. The dull horror he had felt since arriving on the island expanded when he heard what the daily ration for servicemen was. Twelve ounces of bread, six of preserved meat...he was lucky, didn't he know, that today was a Wednesday and would get one and a half tinned sausages. And the first of his three mugs of tea (three!) and it was nectar. The best cup of tea he'd ever had.

Someone pulled out a chair across from him, and he looked up. It was Cocke, who nodded, and set down his own tea. "Morning Clyde."

Edmund nodded, returned the greeting. "Manage to get any sleep?"

Cocke yawned, as if in answer, but did not elaborate. "Marine unit's on stand-down this morning so we're clear to visit. Their Wireless Op wants to check a new VHF on the seaplane tender so we might get a run out in the bay."

"That's good. Thank you. How's the painting?" Edmund said, fishing for a pleasantry.

"I don't do nose art," Cocke snapped. "Nor will I paint a nude, however tasteful, on anyone's barrack block wall."

Edmund started back reflexively. "But I don't want any of that. I'm only here for a couple of weeks!"

Cocke smiled sheepishly. "Sorry, wasn't thinking. I get asked for that sort of stuff a lot."

"I'm genuinely interested," Edmund replied. At that moment, he meant it. He hadn't paid an awful lot of attention to visual arts before, but Cocke's sketches intrigued him.

"Oh. Well." Cocke looked intently at his mug of tea. "I mean. You could have a look at some if you like."

"I'd be delighted to."

"Alright." Cocke was barely less guarded. "This afternoon if we have time

After breakfast they walked the three quarters of a mile from Hal Far to Kalafrana. It was a gentle downhill with the sea spread out around the promontory on which the seaplane base had been built, visible within minutes of leaving the main gate. Edmund had to admit this would be a beautiful spot for a holiday if it weren't for the war. And the infernal heat.

The impression was not dulled on arrival at the station. The breeze was starting to build and the almost-indigo of the bay was studded with sparks as the sun flashed off the ripples. Launches and flying boats bobbed in the rising swell. Edmund felt himself begin to relax despite himself. Cocke introduced him to Flight Lieutenant Thorndike, commander of High Speed Launch 107 which sat, sleek and pugnacious, tied up alongside.

"We fish the gallant fighter boys out of the drink," Thorndike said, "so they may fight, flirt and frolic another day." He gestured at the splinter mat strapped to the front of the wheelhouse. A crest like an RAF squadron badge had been painted at the top, and rows of what looked like kill markings beneath.

"What's this?" Edmund said. "Battle honours?" He peered at the badge, and the motto beneath it: "'The Sea Shall Not Have Them'" he recited.

"I don't see why," Thorndike murmured. "Everyone else has one."

Edmund laughed, before peering sidelong at the officer to check he was supposed to. He looked more closely. They were not kill markings, but little lifebelts. "So, these are all the successful rescues?"

"We don't tend to mention the unsuccessful ones." He grimaced. "I'm not sure we have enough splinter mats to paint those on."

Edmund pursed his lips. He thought of yesterday's flight, the rescue of nothing but a dinghy. "You have an awful lot of sea to cover." He gestured out at the bay. "How on Earth do you find anything out there?"

"It's not just us," Thorndike replied. "There's another boat and crew based at Saint Paul's Bay. But yes, it's a big area. We do what we can."

Nobody said anything for a moment, the only sound was of fenders clonking against the hull as the waves rocked it. "Right." Thorndike clapped his hands and rubbed them.

"Enough moping. It's a lovely day for boating, and we've a wireless to test. Care to join us?"

"Try and stop us," Edmund grinned.

"Right. I'll introduce you to the crew and we can get cracking."

Seaplane Tender 238 was not much more than half the length of the rakish HSL 107, but, Edmund found, was still capable of going at a good lick. He needed a solid handhold as the boat slashed across the swell, barrelling up the waves' long side before bashing into each trough with a hollow thunk. The sound reverberated from stempost to transom, and a hiss of spray flared out like the wings of a bird and disintegrated into the wind, like jewels. Then the launch seemed to shake itself, crouch and leap, like a racehorse after taking a jump.

"Enjoying yourself Lieutenant?" Thorndike shouted, one hand clapped onto his cap, the other hanging onto the cockpit coaming. Fortunately, ST238 had a sunken well-deck aft, sheltered by the 'dog house' forward. If it weren't for that they'd have been soaked within minutes of leaving the quay.

"Yes! Delightful!" he replied. And it was. Just like a run in a powerboat before the war. He'd seen them racing on Windermere in his youth and had always hankered after a spin in one. This was everything he imagined it would be. "Goes at a fair clip, doesn't she?"

"Ah, good. Sure you're alright? There's a bit of a lop on."

"Yes. Fine. Splendid."

Thorndike looked almost disappointed, Edmund thought. He realised that the rest of the crew – the wireless operator, a Maltese called Joe Pace, the gunner, who'd come along for the ride, were peering at him. When he'd ducked into the wheelhouse for a look around, even the coxswain at the wheel had turned to look back every so often, until he caught his eye and his head snapped round again to stare out of the clear-view panel ahead.

"Well. That's good," Thorndike went on. "How about you, Sub Le'tenant Cocke?"

Cocke said something that sounded more like a gulp than words, any sense swallowed up in the growl of the Meadows engines. Edmund turned to look at him. His face was grey, with an odd tint. A second later Cocke lunged for the opposite rail and for a few moments all that was visible of him was his legs, his top half hanging over the cockpit coaming. The rest of him reappeared a little later, as he shuffled backwards into the cockpit.

"Feel better?" Thorndike was stifling a chuckle.

Cocke nodded gingerly.

"You'll get used to it," Thorndike laughed. "One of these days."

Edmund looked at the boat's crew, from face to face. "Oh. You're trying to give us a hard time, aren't you? Sort of...initiation!"

"Just for you old son." Thorndike winked. "We've tormented poor Sub-Lieutenant Cocke on more than one occasion, but he insists on coming back."

"It's your wonderful company, Flight Lieutenant," Cocke deadpanned. In truth, he did look a little better after having heaved his breakfast, such as it was, over the side.

"Cox'n Timms! Two points to port if you please, and throttle back to three-quarters."

The pitch of the engines changed, and the launch's motion immediately became a lot more comfortable.

"So, do all your visitors get a ride on the vomit express? Or just ASR pilots?"

"Just naval types, to be honest with you." Thorndike was suddenly serious. "We got browned off with the Dark Blue treating us as if we weren't proper sailors, so we invited a crowd of them off *Charybdis* for a joyride. They never made fun of us again, I can tell you."

"Took us a day to clean the up-chuck off the boat, but my goodness it was worth it," Joe said, turning back from his radio bench.

Everyone laughed but Cocke started to look a little pale again.

'Patchy', as everyone seemed to call Pace, was talking over the VHF, which seemed to be working satisfactorily. He half turned in his seat and shouted back to those in the cockpit. "Brace yourselves, we're about to get a visit from God."

Edmund frowned at Cocke. "Who...?"

Cocke rolled his eyes. "Who do you think?"

At that moment another note rose over the sound of the Meadows' and a moment later, an aircraft howl-whistled overhead, so low Edmund felt a compulsion to check the mast had not lost the top six inches. The aircraft, a Hurricane, pulled lazily into a climb, banked into a wingover and started an orbit with the launch at the centre, transformed in that moment from a stooping peregrine to a soaring buzzard.

It had happened so suddenly that the idea of diving for the deck had not even flickered into Edmund's thoughts before he knew they were safe. More or less. "Godden," he breathed.

"Thanks, Exile One," Pace could be heard saying from the cabin, "yes I read you. You nearly blew my eardrums out my arse." Everyone sniggered, breaking the tension of the moment a little. As far as their pounding hearts were concerned though, it could have been a Messerschmitt.

Thorndike had collected himself quickly, Edmund noted, which augured well. "You asked how we cover the area," the officer said when he saw Edmund's attention was on him. "We usually get a position, fairly precise. Not always but mostly. But there can be problems with it. We might get the position that a pilot bailed out, which is obviously not going to be exactly where he goes into the drink. The wind can move a dinghy miles from where it was reported. The best thing is if an aircraft can stay overhead until we get there but as I'm sure you can imagine, that's rarely possible."

Edmund nodded. Every drop of fuel in a Spitfire was precious. The amount of time you could stay out over the sea orbiting was strictly limited.

"Let me give you one piece of advice," Thorndike said, his jocularity dropping away again. "If you find yourself lost over the sea or you know you'll run out of fuel before getting back to the island, your instinct will be to try and get as close to home as possible. Don't. Stay where you are and circle, broadcasting for a fix as long as you can. Then, when you do go into the drink, we'll have the clearest possible idea of where you are."

"Alright." Edmund pursed his lips. "Thanks. Fingers crossed it doesn't come to that. What happens if you get to the position and don't find the aircrew?"

"Then we start a search pattern. We call it the square search, as it's exactly that. We sail for a cable's length, then turn ninety degrees to port, and again, and again, and steadily lengthen the legs. In bigger and bigger squares." He smiled tightly. "Of course, if we've got an aircraft co-operating, it's a bit different."

Edmund nodded his agreement. Sailing with the launch had given him an excellent and somewhat sobering sense of how much you could see from a boat like this. Not very much. Especially when there was a sea running. You'd have to keep up a near perfect lookout on all sides, constantly. Even if you were close enough to see something as small as a person clearly, you could easily lose a pilot in a Mae West or a one-man dinghy behind the next crest. It was a sobering realisation. And yet they did pull people out of the water. All those marks on the splinter mat. The system worked. For some people at least. The launch turned back toward Kalafrana.

What had at first seemed a pleasant escape from the war for a few minutes had thrown a shadow. It would be more difficult than he had imagined. He might scour the sea alongside this launch and not save a single life.

No, that would not do. He'd speak to Cocke and Godden, wring from them any tips, anything at all that might make the difference between spotting a speck in an ocean and missing it. For the rest of the trip, he pressed Thorndike on how it was for them to work with an aircraft, which approaches worked best. If he was stuck here, he was going to do the best he could. He made a promise to himself: no airman would be lost if it was in his power to prevent it.

***

That afternoon, Edmund made another familiarisation flight in in one of the rickety Hurricanes, on Cocke's wing this time. He focussed his efforts on spotting anything in the water, as far out as possible. Then remembered the warning he'd been given about the pilots who had been so intent on scanning the sea they didn't see the enemy fighters coming for them.

And concentrating wasn't as easy as all that. As he'd felt during the previous day's flight and the trip on the launch, there was something of the joy of peacetime about the flight, over glittering seas and rugged coast. The little *dghaisa* fishing boats with their high prows and painted eyes like something out of Homer, the arches and sea stacks and island rocks reminding him both of holidays in Cornwall and ancient tales of gods and men. He felt his mind warring between the Mediterranean island paradise that arose from time to time and the ghastly privations and violence that were all too apparent generally. Between wanting to get the hell out, and a tiny part of him that was starting to want to stay here forever.

To his surprise, Cocke did the same as Godden had on the previous day's flight, letting down to deck level before they reached the coast and instigating a nought-feet tailchase over the Maltese landscape. This time was just as nerve-wracking as the last, but for different reasons. There was none of the exhilaration of the follow-my-leader with Godden. Where Godden's flying was assured, imparting confidence to anyone following, Cocke's was erratic, somehow both wild and tentative. Several times he cut across Edmund's path without warning - or appeared to be taking them one way round an obstruction, only to choose the other at the last minute. By the time they turned for home, Edmund was drenched in sweat. It was puddling in his shoes and trickling into his stinging eyes.

Once back on blessed terra firma, he tried to write down something of the experience – the visceral, siren beauty and the ludicrous thrill of the 'beat up', but it would not be hammered into Alexandrines. Frustrated, he laid the writing aside with little more than notes of sensations achieved.

Tomorrow he'd be on the roster for the ASR Flight, and could be called out at any time. He had been lucky so far. It had been quiet, but it was the quiet of held breath. At any time the waves of bombers could return in earnest, the swarms of fighters protecting them, and there would be ditched aviators relying on him.

But before that, he had to face Godden and The Gut, whatever the hell that was. He sought Cocke out for a quiet word and knocked on the door of his cabin. It opened in a waft of turpentine, and something sharper that Edmund couldn't quite identify. Paint, perhaps. He coughed and blinked.

"Sorry," Cocke sniffed, "I try to keep the place ventilated, but it isn't easy."

An easel was set up in the middle of the room with a small canvas on it, a deep blue with a vibrant greenish tinge dominating, a slash of white across it, at the head of which was a leaping launch. Cocke must work fast when the inspiration struck.

"It's nowhere near finished," he sniffed. "Not even sure I will. Just. You know. An idea."

"Yes," Edmund said, thinking of his abortive poetry. "May I look?"

"Not at that one. Ugh. No, let me get some finished ones."

From a wardrobe Cocke produced a bundle of canvases. Edmund was impressed. Here was one of men, RAF and Navy, a mixture of suppressed fear, resignation and defiance on their faces waiting in an air raid shelter. There, a scene from somewhere high up in Valletta, watching battle scarred warships limping into Grand Harbour through a stone arch. A crew climbing into an Albacore under moonlight, determination lining their brows. Soldiers with shovels repairing bomb holes in a runway beneath an incandescent sun. A cargo ship unloaded by yelling stevedores wearing helmets painted like stone paving, their torsos hard and angled as if shaped with an axe. The paintings were not abstract but somehow realer than real. Looking at them, Edmund almost felt he was standing in the scene, trapped in a moment of time like a fly in amber. People's lives framed in a moment. Lives that for the most part might be ended any day, at any moment. It was somehow uplifting and unsettling.

"These are wonderful," Edmund breathed. "You've a talent."

Cocke waved away the compliment. "Amateurish. Clumsy. But it's what I see."

"Hmm. I wouldn't have said so." Anything but that. Yes, there was a slight roughness to them but it was that which gave them their energy. As if the paint itself was not entirely contained. Edmund detected a growing awkwardness from Cocke and remembered the reason he had wanted to talk. "I meant to ask you about 'The Gut'. Godden seems intent on dragging me there. What on Earth is it? A boozer?"

Cocke rolled his eyes. "It's a street. Strait Street. Don't ask me why they call it The Gut. Full of boozers, dancehalls and houses of ill repute. And some places that are all three."

"Oh."

"Not your idea of a good time? No, nor mine. I'd prefer to get quietly blotto somewhere and look at beautiful things, of which Malta is not in short supply. Sadly, there's little of cultural value in Strait Street."

"I wonder if I could get out of it?"

Cocke issued a tired chuckle. "Not likely. When Godden gets an idea into his head..."

At that moment Godden pushed through the door as if the thought had summoned him.

"Come in," Cocke said acidly.

Godden ignored him and looked at Edmund. "Here you are. Ready? Car's outside."

Edmund looked at his watch. Not yet five o'clock. "Bit early isn't it?"

"I've got to see a chap at Lascaris first." He tapped the side of his nose. "You can be having an early one to warm up. And maybe a drink too, *haha*."

Godden practically bundled Edmund into a faded Austin Ten, which set off at a roar signifying a perforated exhaust and juddered along the road towards Valletta.

"There's a reasonable dance place we'll go first," Godden yelled over the stertorous engine. "A couple of the girls aren't bad, but they have a reputation for keeping their legs crossed. You have to either get enough alcohol into them to go with you, or failing that get enough alcohol into you that you can go with one of the others. But you'll be alright. You must have money piled up, being stuck on a carrier for months on end. Jesus, you're lucky you got landed here. Like a holiday really."

A dance place? Girls. Oh Lord. Edmund tried to keep hold of his composure. "I'd really prefer a quiet drink."

"You bloody Brits. You talk like that but get a bit of booze into you and you'll be hanging off the chandelier singing Eskimo Nell and sticking your John Thomas into anything in a skirt."

"I've got a girl. Back home. I shouldn't..." Did he? The Half-Hearted Wren seemed very distant now, but any excuse.

"We've all got girls back home, mate. Trouble is, they're back home and we're here, and trust me, that doesn't help."

Edmund turned in his seat. "Now look here! I gather your squadron gives you a ludicrous amount of latitude but you're a junior officer and I don't care to be spoken to in that manner."

Godden smirked. "And I'm your Flight Leader so we'll call it quits, shall we? By the way, the martinet act really doesn't suit you, old chum." He grinned, wolfishly. "I'm just trying to make sure you have a bit of fun before getting stuck in. Might not get the chance later. C'mon, lighten up. There's enough fluff in Valletta to cover the runway if you lined 'em up and laid 'em down. Phew, wouldn't that be a sight."

Edmund sighed and slumped down in his seat. "Why is this so important to you? Why now?"

Godden was silent for a second, then exhaled through his nose.

"Y'know I said I had plans?"

"I could hardly forget."

"Well it's nothing to do with ASR."

"Oh?"

"Mike said you'd talked to him about the bomb racks on the Hurris."

Bomb racks? What did that have to do with anything? "Yes. For long range tanks or dinghy packs, he said."

Godden chuckled. "Poor Mike. No, there's no way we'll get tanks or dinghies, none at all. No, I want to hang bombs off 'em."

Edmund turned to look at Godden. Was this some sort of joke that he hadn't cottoned on to? Like the initiation on the boat? "Bombs? Why? You're an ASR flight."

"That's strictly a temporary measure. Anyway, as you saw, we're on a hiding to nothing. We aren't achieving a bloody thing. But we could."

Edmund resisted the urge to snort. They were saving lives. That wasn't nothing. "I've been in the drink," he said. "Let me tell you. What we're doing has value."

"A drop in the ocean," Godden sneered. "So to speak. And what's it for? Mostly pilots who are trying to stop the Jerries from bombing us. Well what if we can stop 'em getting shot down in the first place?"

None of this made sense. Perhaps Godden was undergoing some kind of breakdown. "How do you propose to do that with bombs?"

"Sicily," Godden declared, like it was the punchline to a favourite joke. "More specifically, the airfields."

Edmund laughed bitterly. Godden was insane. It was the only explanation. "Don't we already have bombers hitting the airfields?"

"Pfft." Godden shook his head. "They don't dare. Not for months. Too *dangerous*."

"Ha!" Edmund huffed in disbelief. "You don't think that tells you something?"

"No, no, no." Godden smacked the steering wheel with each syllable. "Of course it's dangerous for Blenheims. Everything's dangerous for bloody Blenheims. No. We go in, on the deck, at high speed. Drop a few two-fifty pounders, blow up some hangars, shoot 'em up a bit, do whatever damage we can, leave them in complete disarray and hightail it back towards Malta. They go struggling into the air after us. And then run slap-bang into a posse of Spits waiting there for the exact purpose! It can't fail!"

Edmund closed his eyes. The world seemed to be swaying around him and there was a hard knot in his midriff. "I assure you. It can. Fighter sweeps are like playing roulette. What happens if you end up missing your escort? Or something happens to them on the way and they don't make the rendezvous?" Like those poor bastards in Skuas whose RAF escort had never appeared and left them in the lurch over Norway. Even the huge wings of Spits and Hurris, carved to bits as they'd tried to take the fight into France in forty-one. The stories he'd heard when he was in training. A shudder ran through him. "It's not worth the gamble."

"Well." Godden took his eyes off the road for longer than Edmund would have liked, just to glare at him. "I thought better of you. You're a fighter pilot aren't you?"

"Exactly. A fighter pilot. Not a bomber pilot. Not a ground attack pilot... Wait, is that what your ludicrous low-level stunts after ASR flights are for? Practice?"

"Spot on. What, you just thought they were hi-jinks?"

"Well..."

Godden shook his head, chuckling. "You did. You thought 'that Godden's always larking about and he's burning up valuable petrol for a wheeze.' Well, let me tell you, I'm as serious about winning this war as anyone, and I don't intend to wait for permission from Their Lordships to do something that'll help."

"Well that's to your credit, but we can't all run off and try to win the war our own way, can we?"

"Think what you like chum, this raid is going ahead."

"I can't see Commander Haynes agreeing to it."

Godden laughed, and there was triumph in the sound. "Already has. We just need old Hugh-Pugh up at Lascaris to sign it off and a Spit squadron or two to step up. I've been sounding them out. We'll get our Spits, never you worry."

"I'm sorry, I can't agree to do it."

To his surprise, Godden didn't protest. He just nodded. "You'll come around," Godden said after a moment, almost more as though he was talking to himself than Edmund. "You're a warrior. Not a glorified swimming pool lifeguard. I've got your number. You'll come around."

There was no way on Earth Edmund was going to change his mind. It was a death sentence, a waste of good men and machines. He sat back, confident that nobody in the high command could possibly sanction such folly. Even in this upside-down place. At the speed Godden was driving they were nearing the outskirts of Hamrun already, and low buildings were visible over the dry stone walls. They had to drive through it, then Floriana before they got to Valletta though in reality the cities had grown into one another and it was all built-up from here.

There was something wrong. At first Edmund thought the engine was making an unhealthy noise but it was coming from somewhere else. He put his head out of the window and looked up, then back. Blazes! "Get off the road," he yelled, "there's a One-Oh-Nine behind us!"

Godden glanced in the mirror. "Nah, can't be. It's a Spit beating us up."

"I tell you, it's-"

A deep clatter scored the air. Cannon fire! The car swerved and Edmund was thrown against the door. For a moment he thought Godden was pulling off the road – thank goodness, they could dive behind a wall and... But no, the car shimmied, straightened and continued forward. Godden dropped gear, the engine howled and the Austin picked up speed.

"What the hell are you doing? Get off the road!" Edmund shrieked, but Godden was intent on the road and the mirror. More gunfire blasted out, Edmund saw the puffs in the road ahead where machine gun rounds were striking, then a resounding *clang!* reverberated around the interior. They'd been hit...not too badly it seemed. The growl of the engine swelled and bellowed overhead.

Edmund chanced another look. "He's coming round again. What are you doing?"

"Getting amongst the buildings, he can't hit us there," Godden replied, with icy calm.

"There are civvies in there!"

"That's their bloody problem."

"Godden!"

The engine raced and the car slithered from left to right, weaving across the road. They were almost among the buildings now.

"Godden, stop it!" Jesus, there were civilians there, women, children! He should stop this. Could make a grab for the steering wheel... Go on...go on... But his arm would not move to wrest control away from Godden and they were in a street, a long, straight, wide street with little cover and the Messerschmitt was still coming, the guns rattling, the bullet strikes flashing all around them. Then, a vicious *bang* from somewhere in the car and the Austin was lurching one way then the other, another *bash* as a front wheel hit something, they seemed to be flying sideways... *Crunch*, finishing in a xylophone of smashed glass, and Edmund felt himself in free air, tumbling, then rolling on the ground, a football with limbs.

He had no recollection of closing his eyes, but he must have done as they opened and he found himself staring upwards into a pair of deep brown eyes. He must be dreaming of course because it was the woman from Valletta and that couldn't be... "Have you come to tell me to get to a shelter?" he said. "I promise I'll go this time."

"Are you hurt?" she said. "Were you shot?"

"No. No, I don't think so." He was suddenly aware of his body. He didn't seem to be in any pain at all, which was strange. He moved to sit up and- "Aargh! Good God." Sharp, burning, everywhere. It hurt to breathe, move, lie still.

"There's no need to take His name in vain," the woman said. "And you haven't been shot. Can you stand?"

Shot? The Messerschmitt! What had happened to the Messerschmitt? He tried to listen for the engine but there was only whistling in his ears. "The One-Oh-Nine. The aeroplane that attacked us. Is it...?"

"Gone."

Against the burning, every muscle screaming, he put his palms on the ground and pushed himself up. "I was in a car." The last few seconds...something he couldn't remember. "I don't know how I..."

"Yes. The car crashed. You were thrown out. There."

It must have only just happened. Steam was still pouring from the wrecked radiator of the Austin. The bonnet was askew, shunted into a vee. There were two large, ragged holes in the back of the saloon, and the whole affair was jammed against the wall of a building.

"Godden!" he yelped. "My...um, comrade. Driving the car."

"We're getting him out," the woman said. Calm. She was calm.

He staggered towards the car, a couple of steps. "Is he alright?" A couple more steps. There were civilians clustered around the door. They parted to let him see. He stooped to see inside. "Godden, are you alright?"

"Fine. Fine." He sounded more annoyed than hurt. "Cut my bloody leg open. And the steering column's trapping my goddamned foot."

"You should tell your...comrade about the Lord's name too, yes?"

Edmund nodded, making the street around him spin. "Sorry. We'll try to be more...um, respectful."

"Good. That is good."

The men gathered around the door again. Someone ran up with a saw, which was passed, person to person, into the press. In a moment the sound of blade on metal could be heard, screeching into the street.

"Be bloody careful for sparks," Godden's voice echoed out of the car, "there's petrol down there."

"I'll speak to Sub-Lieutenant Godden about his language." Edmund avoided the woman's gaze, but glanced at her. Tall. Upright. Older. In her thirties, perhaps, even early forties. It was the same woman. He was sure of it. It wasn't just that he was so unfamiliar with Maltese women that they all looked alike. He grimaced at the thought. Her voice, though. He'd never forget that.

"Good. Such things might not be important where you come from but they are to me. I am Liena Ganado. I will see that you are taken to the hospital at Imtarfa but first you must come to the casualty station."

"Lina, thank you-"

"Liena."

"Liena. I'm Edmund. Clydesdale. People call me Clyde."

"Clyde? Like the river?"

"Yes, I suppose."

And then as he turned to look at Liena, she had turned to look at him and as their eyes engaged it was like a switch being thrown in Edmund's innards. Just a look but it felt like a punch. He felt suddenly vulnerable, naked under that gaze. And oh God, she was smiling. He should turn to water and run through the cracks in the paving. This was wrong. He should not be here. He should go back to Hal Far and never think of this woman again. He smiled back.

"Thank you, Liena. I'm sorry we put you to the trouble."

She shrugged. "They send their fighters over to machine gun anyone they find in the open. You should have stopped the car and hidden behind a wall."

"Yes, yes. Next time. Definitely." The agony in his muscles had subsided. He looked at his limbs, his torso. His uniform was scuffed and torn. His hands were grazed and the cuts full of grit. His knees had taken a bit of a knock by the feel of them. But he was sure he wasn't badly hurt.

"Give me your hand," Liena said. Meekly, without knowing what she intended, he extended his right, as if to shake hands. Briskly, she turned it flat and began dabbing at it, none too gently, with a dampened pad. He tried not to wince. She sloshed some water from a flask over the cloth, rinsing blood and dirt away, and carried on. "The heel of the hand always is hurt worst," she said as she worked. "When you are thrown or fall, you put your arm out like this-" she extended her own to demonstrate "-and the heel hits the ground first. You can also break your collarbone that way. Are you sure you aren't hurt here-" she pointed "-when you move your shoulder?"

Edmund tentatively rotated his shoulder. There was no additional pain.

"Do it again," she said, and surprisingly, delightfully, rested the side of her head against his shoulder. He felt the warmth of her as he rocked his shoulder gently.

"Fine." She moved away again. "You would hear the bone scraping if you'd broken it."

He shuddered at that and then felt a momentary awkwardness. "I think I'm OK. I shouldn't need to go to the hospital."

She glanced at him. "You should come to the casualty station. Those hands should be cleaned properly and dressed."

Just then the steering column succumbed to the saw and the civilians extracted Godden like a rotten tooth. Despite loud and sometimes blasphemous protestations, he was placed in a stretcher and the party began moving up the road. Edmund fell in beside Liena.

"Ah, Miss Ganado." His face was burning hot with what he was about to do. Surely his lifelong lethargy would prevent him... The constant inability to act when it counted.

She looked at him, waiting for him to speak, frowning slightly when he didn't.

"I'd like to take you out," he blurted. "To say thank you."

Liena stared at him, eyes wide, and oh God he'd made a dreadful mistake, but then she laughed and it was worse. His gut twisted. "Lieutenant. Edmund? There are plenty of girls your own age in Valletta."

He ignored the heat in his cheeks, the sense that his face must be crimson. "It's not about...*that*. I...feel. I want to. And for the last time we met, which you probably don't remember, but you tried to tell me to go to a bomb shelter in Valletta and I didn't and it was b-... It was extremely stupid of me. So this is the second time you've helped me. Tried to, anyway."

"I remember." She raised an eyebrow. "It's good that you survived. The Lord has given you another chance. You should use it well."

"I intend to. So could I...erm..." Oh Lord, what now? She didn't seem like the kind of woman one could take to a bar. Pictures, maybe? "Er, visit you... Do you like films?"

Liena turned to him again, appraising. She said nothing.

"I'm only here for a few weeks," he said. "And if you don't want to, I shan't bother you any more. But if there's something nice I can do for you to thank you..."

She shrugged. "It's what I'm meant to do."

Edmund thought that was going to be the end of it, when Liena said "Alright. Tomorrow evening. Six O'clock. Meet me by the Kingsgate. Bring a Thermos of coffee."

"Alright, I'll be there."

"...And a clean handkerchief."

***

Edmund went with Godden to the casualty station at Hamrun and saw him to the hospital at Imtarfa. His right calf had been sliced open and there was a small piece of shrapnel from a cannon shell in the wound which would probably need to be extracted by a surgeon but it wasn't too bad and the nurses said he'd be fit to fly in a few days.

Godden was furious to miss his meeting at Lascaris – he would not tell Edmund what it was about or who it was with, though Edmund suspected it was connected to his ludicrous scheme to bomb Sicilian airfields with clapped-out Hurricanes. Godden was even more furious to have missed out on a night in Valletta. Most of all he was furious to be stuck in a hospital bed for a couple of days – days! – and certain that the idiots left in charge would have ruined his small command by the time he was able to return and reclaim it. With a long exhalation and a new sense of calm, Edmund left the pilot to the mercy of the hospital, or possibly the other way round, and cadged a lift back to Hal Far.

Godden's absence meant that for a couple of days, he and Cocke would need to share the ASR duties between them but that did not seem too onerous given the light number of callouts. The thought of the meeting with Liena – not a date exactly, whatever it was – brought a feeling of lightness too, even though he was determined not to allow it to affect his concentration in the air.

One dark knot within the new sense of contentment was the aircraft that had shot him up. If it was what he thought it was – no, not thought, *knew* – it meant the Luftwaffe was back. He was convinced it was an Me109 but Godden had refused to believe it. "Must have been a Macchi," he insisted. "And you just misidentified it. That bloody awful eyesight of yours, it's a wonder you saw it at all."

He told Haynes as soon as he got back to the station, and Haynes was of the same view as Godden. "Hmm. Recce flights don't show any sign of Jerries coming back to Sicily. Or any sort of build-up. Could have been a one-off I suppose. Or maybe the Eyeties are flying Messerschmitts now. They've had some Stukas for a while. Even though it is unusual for the Eyeties to go free-ranging like that, it doesn't seem likely. Are you sure it wasn't a Macchi? Or a Reggiane?"

He was sure, but then these people had been on Malta far longer than he, and seemed to think it was doubtful to suspect was a 109. Reluctantly he concluded that aircraft recognition in the heat of the moment was an inexact science, and he had probably got it wrong.

He had not taken over as duty pilot for long when there was a call-out. A Spit pilot gone into the sea off Zonqua Point, and as there were some plots on the grid – albeit well to the North – the controller decided to request a pair of Hurricanes just to be on the safe side.

The two fighters climbed into the hard blue above Malta, sun glinting off chips in the drab grey paint on their wings. Cocke was flying lead, Edmund tail-end charlie. Edmund grudgingly accepted the arrangement made sense, though he would have liked more practice at searching the sea. The site of the ditched Spit was not far off the coast, though it was on the other side of the island to Kalafrana, so it would take the launch a little while to catch up with them. They crossed the island's East coast after a few minutes and cruised on to the position. There was nothing immediately below, so they started a search pattern.

After no more than ten minutes, the radio fizzed and Edmund heard Cocke say "I see Fluoroscene dye." His heart pounded. Success? He chanced a look, tearing his eyes away from the search for enemy aircraft for a second. A bizarrely regular circle of bright pea-green sat among the deeper blue. Edmund forced himself to slow his breathing, return his attention to the skies again. Cocke turned, lining them up to pass over the patch of dye again."

After another couple of minutes, he reported "there's the dinghy. Someone in it. Looks alive." He radioed the position to control.

"Good work Exile Leader," a plummy voice boomed out in the speakers. "Vector three-five-five to return to base."

Edmund frowned. Return so early? And that course was to the north. Had he misunderstood where they were? Three-five-five would take them to...

His headphones crackled again and he heard a familiar rasp shouting "No, no, no! Ignore that last message Exile Flight. Maintain station!"

"Some joker in Sicily, Exile Two," Cocke added. "They try it on now and again. Must think we're green."

Edmund felt a plunging in his midriff. Did that mean the Italians knew where they were? They must know this was an ASR flight... It was dislocating. If the Italians were trying to steer them north, that would put them down-sun of an enemy formation approaching from...there!

A string of particles against the azure, almost beyond seeing. "Bandits, two o'clock, high," he radioed as calmly as possible. In the seconds it had taken him to do so, he recognised the typical echelon formation of the Regia Aeronautica. Not Jerries, then... Almost certainly fighters. "I see six."

"Understood. Should we break?"

Edmund kept his eyes on the aircraft. They weren't being bounced. The Eyeties looked as though they were orbiting themselves. "No. Not yet. Be ready to make a break for it." There were too many of them to fight. They had worked a little closer though were still circling. A little higher but not so much as to confer any real advantage. Long, pointed noses. Macchis, the newer ones. MC.202s. They were thoroughly outmatched. He listened to the controller. "Hello Exile Leader, Exile Leader, am vectoring a squadron of Spits to your position. Should be with you in four or five minutes."

Edmund held his breath for a moment - and reached a decision. "Hello Exile Leader, recommend we reverse course," he said, heart catching in his throat, "to avoid being cut off. But we can stay in the vicinity. I don't think they're interested in us."

There was a pause, long enough that Edmund had time to wonder if Cocke's wireless had failed. Then, "I'm not sure Clyde, I think there's a problem with my kite. The oil pressure seems awfully low. We should head back. The launch knows the position, and the Spits are on the way."

"What's it reading? The oil pressure."

Cocke told him. It was a bit low but not drastically. These engines weren't exactly in their prime.

"That's alright. Keep an eye on it."

"But what if we get into a dogfight? I don't know if it can take full throttle."

Edmund looked back towards the Macchis. They were reversing course, keeping their distance but not turning tail. The Eyeties might just be looking for their own ditched airmen. Or they might be waiting until any witnesses departed so they could shoot up the dinghy unseen. Or worse, the launch. No, he would not chance it and leave the men down there unprotected.

"You stay here, orbit above the dinghy and keep broadcasting to the launch," he said. "I'll stay between them and you. If they try to interfere or work round to cut us off, I'll keep 'em occupied for a bit. Just stay on that dinghy."

"Understood."

"Trust me."

"OK."

Cocke didn't sound happy about it. At least if his engine did fail, he could ditch beside the launch. But Edmund did not think it would fail. He'd flown enough hours on Hurricanes by now to know when one was likely to pack up.

Edmund tipped the Hurricane into a bank, and the fighter curved away from the other, then back to take up a parallel course. His peripheral vision was hooked on two points. The group of Italian fighters to starboard, and the other Hurricane hovering over the downed airman to port. And then there were three points. Damn it. One of the Macchis had detached.

Edmund gently increased the throttle to full, not slamming it open – that would be a dead giveaway, with a tell-tale puff of black smoke from the exhausts – and pitching the nose up a little just to keep his height on a level with the Macchi. It was approaching on a beam course... Edmund turned into him a little, not dramatically... The Italian was not obviously setting up for an attack, but with these Eyeties, who could ever say what they were up to?

The Macchi kept drawing closer, closer. The pilot had tweaked his course ever so slightly and would now pass slightly behind Edmund. Damn. Edmund's heart rate kicked up a gear and he turned into the Macchi a little more. Then the Macchi changed course again, and Edmund decided.

A kick of rudder and a pull of aileron, then back on the stick and the Hurricane was turning hard, down, below the nose of the Macchi. Thinking back to Madagascar, the French fighters bouncing them...could not get a bead if he just kept turning hard...

A second later Edmund was cursing himself for an idiot as he caught a glimpse of the Macchi carving upwards, into a barrel roll, perfectly placed to drop in on his tail. Damn, damn, damn! He pulled into a left turn, into the Macchi's turn, blazing with hope that he could stay far enough ahead, that the gunfire would all fall behind...but the Hurricane was running out of momentum, and if he kept this up he'd stall before much longer. There was a mass bearing down on his chest, he fought it, fought to lift his ribs to let some air into his lungs. Blood was pushing at his vision. The Hurricane was starting to twitch. He heaved his head around to look for the Macchi, and... Joy! The fighter had tried to follow him into the turn, but was carrying too much speed, sliding out wide! Edmund rolled level for a second, just enough to pick up a bit of speed, then pulled into a turn to the right. The Macchi was level, almost ahead, and still slicing round to the left. A little further and Edmund could get on his tail... The blood was pumping, triumphant but damn it, the Italian flipped his fighter through the vertical just as Edmund reversed his turn again. Now they were weaving around each other, trying to force their guns to bear, never quite succeeding...

Edmund held the Hurricane into the turn, reversing it whenever the Italian did. Hands beginning to cramp...he stared at the flap lever, not daring to release a hand from the spade grip. Dump a bit of flap and fall in behind...but then he'd be easy meat if one of the other Macchis decided to join in. A wash of ice over his skin...he was a dead man if they did. He knew Cocke would be no help, even if he tried to. As if the urgency of his thoughts had made some psychic connection, he heard Cocke radioing "*Control, where the hell are those Spits*?" and giving an updated position. The message sounded as though it was being shouted in a gale, or pounding surf. He did not hear the response.

They were at minimum speed now, balancing on the edge of the stall, turning as hard as they dared. Daring too much. Edmund felt the Hurricane's turn tightening again, swallowing its own tail, seconds from falling out of the sky. He braced his arms against the stick. They were losing height too. The waves were there, just below the wingtip. Good God, another thirty seconds and he'd go in. Twenty. Last chance. He rolled level, lunged across the cockpit and heaved the flap lever. The warning siren shrilled in his ears, and he pulled the gear down too, listening as the wheels clunked down, swinging his head from side to side, rolling his last hope up into a ball and grasping it. Overshoot, damn you, overshoot!

If the Italian didn't anticipate the sudden slowing, he would barrel past, Edmund would have a chance. If he did anticipate, Edmund was already dead. The sound of his own breathing was deafening.

A second passed. Two. The Macchi did not appear, booming, glowering, vast in his canopy. He glanced to either side – nothing – and then the mirror.

The Macchi was sitting behind him, nose high, flaps down. Edmund closed his eyes. He had enough time for a twinge of unformed regret, attached to nothing in particular, and then-

Nothing happened.

He opened his eyes again. The Italian fighter was moving aside, drawing level. It eased up, wingtip to wingtip. The pilot slid back the canopy panel, unbuttoned his oxygen mask, and turned to look at Edmund. He was grinning. Then he waved, saluted, closed the canopy side, and the Macchi peeled away.

Edmund let out a kind of bark. His hands, arms, legs vibrated. They would not do anything he wanted. And then, gradually, control returned, his hands through the shaking answered his thoughts. He retracted the undercarriage, raised the flaps. And only then became aware of a voice in his ears. "...Exile Two, come in! Exile Two, reverse course for heaven's sake, Clyde. You're flying toward Sicily! The launch has made the pickup, the Spits'll be here any moment! The Eyeties are going."

A voice that did not sound like his own quavered a response. Arms that felt full of molten lead banked the Hurricane into a wide, gentle turn.

***

Edmund had only the dimmest memories of flying back to Hal Far, landing, all the myriad bits and pieces he needed to work through after a flight. He only began to come back to himself when he had to complete a combat report. It took some resolve not to write simply 'hooked by Italian and thrown back like an undersized trout'.

He wanted to sleep. To collapse into bed and oblivion, but he had promised to meet Liena this evening. His stomach lurched. Heavens, what was he playing at? It was foolishness. Idiocy. But he had made the arrangement. He could not simply fail to turn up. That would be the height of bad manners. In a daze, he prepared for the evening, trying to make himself presentable. And what was it she'd requested? A thermos of coffee... And a clean handkerchief? She must have her reasons, he supposed, though it felt a little like something out of a folk tale. The hero charged with finding a succession of ever more bizarre objects to win the princess.

The station Austin had been wrecked when Godden crashed it, so there was no alternative to the bus. It was frightfully delayed and even with the time he had allowed, Edmund was nearly a quarter of an hour late as he hurried towards the Kingsgate. At least it was easy enough to find. But would she still be there? No, he was late. She would have had every right to expect he would be there at Six, already waiting, and to leave after a couple of minutes. His mind started to tussle between crushing disappointment and relief.

As Edmund approached the gate, over the bridge from the Floriana side, there was no sign of her. The warring disappointment and relief increased in pitch. He walked under the gate. And there she was, in the shade, and wearing cotton short-sleeved dress with a knee-length skirt of the same kind that every woman or girl over the age of six seemed to wear here, in slightly faded dark blue, and a funny sort of sunhat on her head. His pace increased, almost involuntarily, like the broad stupid grin he could feel plastered to his face and could do nothing about. But hold on, that wasn't a sunhat. It was a tin helmet! And it had three letters painted on it. A...R...

Oh. Of course. She was an Air Raid Warden. She even had an armband.

That explained demanding he went to a shelter. Giving first aid. Helping a rescue party.

Of course. He felt like slapping himself on the forehead in the middle of the street. How had he not realised?

She noticed him, watched him approach. Did not wave or smile or even nod. Oh dear.

"Hello," he said as he stood before her. "Sorry I'm late. The bus. I'm still getting used to how things work round here."

Those eyes. Edmund struggled to return her gaze, swallowed in vulnerability again. As though one word from her and he would be undone, destroyed. This is how moths feel when they fly into a candle, he thought. Exultant. Vindicated. Lost.

"Did you bring the thermos?" she asked.

"Yes." He produced it. "And the handkerchief, but-"

"Well that's something. Come on. Let's find somewhere to sit."

Edmund had been so focussed on Liena that he had not fully taken in the scene inside the gate. A row of grand buildings stretched away along a ruler-straight street that was now like a gap-toothed mouth. Spaced yawned where once buildings had stood, heaped with rubble. On the right, magnificent pillars speared towards the empty sky, the roof that they had once borne now tumbled around their bases.

As if it was the most normal thing in the world, Liena walked towards the ruin, found a large block of stone that rested, its top almost level, almost bench-height, and sat on it.

There was only one cup on the thermos so they shared it, tipping a few mouthfuls of coffee into it, drinking, passing it back to the other. Edmund didn't tend to drink coffee but found himself enjoying the potency of it.

"Have you lived in Valletta all your life?" he asked.

"No," she said. "Only since the war."

"And the..." he gestured at the tin helmet and the armband. "Air-raid precautions?"

"Also since the war."

"Oh. Yes." He felt his cheeks colouring.

Liena smiled. "When Italy declared war, the governor asked for volunteers. I had no other responsibilities. My mother can look after herself. So I came to work in Valletta."

"How come you were in Hamrun when we crashed the car?"

"The ARP headquarters is there. There was a briefing. You chose a good time and place to crash."

"I shall send my thanks to the enemy," Edmund deadpanned.

Liena smiled patiently. She took off the tin hat, revealing dark brown hair, a few strands of grey running through it, tied back, and began to tell him about her air raid work. Simple, mundane even. But crucial.

He glanced at her sidelong. Tried not to let his gaze linger as she spoke. Failed. Her face was rather long, with a pointed chin, her nose a little large. She was starting to develop lines around her mouth and eyes. She might look hard were it not for those eyes, soft with understanding one moment, sparking with humour the next. It hardly mattered how she looked. She was exceptionally beautiful.

"And," he said before he could stop himself, "you aren't married?"

She looked at him levelly, a mix of disappointment and long-suffering in her eyes. "No. I was never married."

Edmund looked at his shoes. "Sorry. I didn't mean to pry."

"It's alright. The truth is, I never really had the choice."

"No?"

"Someone's mother decided they didn't like the look of me." She shrugged. "It happens. You do something, you don't even know what, or maybe nothing, people whisper, and before you know it, the whole village thinks it of you. I am 'too dark'. I am 'like a Turk'. They forbid their sons from having anything to do with me. It means I am...how would you say it? A bad influence."

"That's terrible!"

She looked at him, sidelong. "And now here I am, sitting on a street corner, drinking coffee with an Englishman. Perhaps they were right."

Edmund's mouth fell open. He jumped to his feet, babbling apologies. Liena fixed him with a glare for a moment and then laughed.

"I'm joking. A bit. Anyway, I didn't mind. It meant I could do what I wanted, more or less. I might not have got to come to Valletta, be an ARP warden, with a husband deciding for me. And I never particularly wanted children. I'm glad I don't have any now. The worry that parents must suffer as the bombs fall! I pray for them, daily. And I thank God I don't have their burden. It is for the best."

"Ah. Yes." Edmund nodded, looked at his feet again. He knew nothing about this island, its people. He felt exposed again. A lost child.

"The other day, when you said God had given me a second chance?" Edmund blurted. "I think He definitely did today." He told her about the dogfight, the Italian pilot who had the drop on him but had let him go. It still felt unreal. A dream.

Liena smiled, openly this time. "You are beginning to see, I think."

Edmund did not know what he could see at all, but smiled and nodded. They finished the coffee, and Liena led them to a water pump, sluiced out the flask and filled it with water. Smiling, she handed it back to him without offering a word in explanation.

After they'd started back up towards the bombed opera house – apparently that was what the grand building on Strada Reale was – Liena said "Now, if you like, you can accompany me on my rounds."

"Of course," he replied. She handed him her tin helmet and slipped her arm through his. He thought his joy would burn him up. It should radiate through his skin like a searchlight. How could these people around not see it?

Liena's 'rounds' were of this part of Valletta's air-raid shelters, of which there far more than Edmund imagined an area that small could contain. Storerooms, cellars, rough caves scooped out of the ground for the purpose. A fair few were in the vaults of churches, which, Edmund realised, was one of the only things Valletta seemed to have in abundance. It was cooler below ground than outside, the air moist. He had a sensation of crypts, which he must have visited as a child but had no memory of.

There were plenty of people already in them. Whole families, with beds and other furniture in alcoves scooped out of the bedrock. She moved through the shelters, exchanging a word here and there with the occupants, in Maltese or English, checking everyone had what they might need to get through a night in the bunker, that lamps had fuel, first-aid kits were properly stocked...

Edmund marvelled once again at her composure. They all knew her, admired her, he could see. He experienced a moment's idiotic pride that he was her companion on this evening, holding her tin hat and flask, like a schoolboy carrying a classmate's books. Sweet lunacy!

"More and more people are living in the shelters now," she explained when they were back in the cooling street. "Their homes have been bombed. There is nowhere else for them go but underground. Below the surface the rock is quite soft. They have been allowed to dig out their own spaces, to bring in whatever furniture they can."

"In England," he said, "the government was worried that if people spent too much time in air raid shelters, they'd never come out."

Liena laughed. "That's stupid. Who would want to stay underground when they don't have to?"

"Yes, quite." He looked around. All the people still going on with their lives. Knowing that sooner or later – and probably sooner – there would be bombs falling from the sky once again. It was miraculous. At one point they moved past the end of Strait Street, raucous, frenetic, packed with sailors and soldiers slithering from bar to bar. He did not regret missing out.

Edmund noticed several other ARP wardens doing similar work to Liena. Mostly men, but a few women.

Then through high-walled, narrow streets – perhaps the same ones he had wandered through on his arrival – beneath the cupola of a church, round a corner, another larger church, with a dome and bell towers. They stopped, and Edmund noticed they were back near the opera house. The sky had lost its steel, was softening to pastel shades. He looked at his watch and was amazed to see that it was nearly eight o'clock. "What now?" he asked.

Liena rolled her eyes - but smiled. "Do you have somewhere to be, Lieutenant?"

"Nowhere I'd rather be," he replied, altogether too serious, and she laughed again. Again, it was like a punch.

"Now I'm just waiting for the bombers to come," she said.

Edmund exhaled slowly. Bombers. He tried to smile. "Let's hope they take the night off."

"They won't." She looked at him, head tilted, for a moment, and seemed to come to some decision. "We have time. Follow me."

She led Edmund upward, between two churches – "Our Lady of the Victories, and Saint Catherine of Italy," Liena said, gesturing to each.

"I favour the former, should the need arise," Edmund murmured. Liena looked at him with great forbearance. The harbour was visible ahead, far below. And suddenly, amidst this war-ravaged city, they were in a garden. A tiny splinter of paradise, partitioned on two sides with an arched wall.

"Come on," said Liena, and walked through an arch. Edmund found himself on a paved terrace, perched on the top of a cliff, the harbour hundreds of feet below.

The war had touched this place, as it had everywhere else. Further along, the terrace and the outer arches disappeared into a yawning void. Edmund edged closer. Through the gap he could see a lower terrace – intact, but what had once been part of the gardens was now the site of a medium anti-aircraft battery. The dark barrels of the Bofors cannon jutted at the sky like a warning.

"There are the Three Cities," Liena said, pointing out across the harbour. "Bormla, L-Isla and Il-Birgu."

"What's the fort on Il...Il-Birgu?" There was a vast, stepped fortification projecting out into the water. It looked indestructible.

"Fort Saint Angelo. It was once known as The Castle of the Sea."

"I can see why."

"And speaking of forts, just below us, down there, see?...is Lascaris Bastion. In case you should need to run there in the middle of an air raid."

Edmund glanced at Liena, who was suppressing a smirk.

Darkness was falling. They stood, sometimes chatting, sometimes in silence, watching the sun set over the city. It was like a balm. Nevertheless, Edmund felt his heart began to beat faster. This time, it was nothing to do with Liena's presence. The bombers would be here soon. He wondered if he should try to get back to the airfield, but in his mind had already committed to seeing this out with Liena. As long as he was back before the morning's roll-call he wouldn't be in breach of regs. Assuming there was anything left of him to return to Hal Far.

The Western horizon was still stained rose when the Rediffusion speakers started up. From the gardens, high above the city, they could hear the echoing phrases, slightly out of sync, jarring. *Air Raid Warning, Air Raid Warning, Air Raid Warning*, and then again in Maltese. A few moments later, the air raid sirens began to wail, starting somewhere over the other side of the city and then creeping closer.

Edmund glanced at Liena but she seemed frozen to the spot. He could not help but to look out across the harbour as the first searchlight beams slashed into the sky, and then the first distant ack-ack guns *thu-thumped*, the sound more in Edmund's chest than his ears, and Liena turned to him.

"We have work to do."

They hurried back down into the city. The streets were clearing fast, but whenever Liena saw anyone who looked as though they were lingering, or didn't know where they were going, and directed them to the nearest shelter. Wherever they were, she instantly knew the closest bunker and the best way to get there. Edmund followed, feeling helpless.

And then they were the last people out in the open, or so it felt. "Alright, we've done all we can do until the raid's over," Liena panted. "We should get to shelter ourselves. Come on." The guns had risen to a *fortissimo*, and the first thuds of concussion signalled bombs were falling.

The shelter Liena chose was the vault of a church – he did not ask which – and it was already somewhat crowded. Iron beds lined the walls and people had spread rugs on the stone floor. The sounds of the air raid were muffled but not shut out. It might be a thunderstorm but could never be mistaken for that. The tattoo was too regular.

And it was closer. Edmund felt himself tense, hunched down, knowing the blow was coming, but, Christ! – the whole room juddered – it was still a shock when it did.

Edmund coughed – everyone around was coughing. The air was clogged with dust.

"Handkerchief!" Liena yelled in his ear. Dumbly he pulled it from his pocket and handed it to her. Then "Flask!" and he handed that over too. Liena splashed some water over the cloth, folded it in half, then held it up to his face and tied it over his mouth and nose. She pulled out a cloth of her own, wet it, and he helped tie it on although he sensed she could do it just as easily by herself.

"Take these," she said, pulling a pile of bandages from a first aid kit and shoving them at him. Edmund followed her around the shelter, helping anyone who didn't have their own cloth, and then, when everyone was attended to, giving sips of water to anyone who had none.

It was a struggle to breathe freely with the wet cloth over his face, but far better than heaving all that dirt into your lungs. Several times, just as the air had begun to clear, the walls shook as a bomb hit nearby, and fresh dust bloomed out from the old stone.

Had the tempo of the bombs decreased? Edmund tried to time the gaps. It did seem that there were fewer of them now.

And then the world ripped apart. Roaring. Dust cascaded from above, below, beside, stone crunched and creaked. He stretched out an arm to find Liena, her arm was groping back towards him, and he rushed into it. They clung to each other as if the world was falling to pieces around them and they were the only safe things left. He felt her face buried in his neck, the bones in her arms pressing into the recesses between his ribs. Whatever happened in the next few seconds, minutes, hours, it would be OK.

Week 2

23 June 1942

The next morning, Edmund wrote to Barbara, his half-hearted Wren girlfriend, to tell her she should consider herself free – he used those words, *you should consider yourself free*, having run through a bewildering sequence of phrases, none of which managed to say what he wanted to without sounding either cruelly brusque or pathetically sentimental. She would be upset, he knew. Not for losing him – he didn't suppose for a moment she would consider that any loss at all – but for the decision not being hers. As he realised this, he knew parting with her was the right course. He didn't mention Liena, of course. There was nothing to mention; they had no understanding and Edmund expected nothing from that quarter, though she was undoubtedly the reason. Edmund could not hold even the light, casual affection for Barbara in his heart at the same time as the glorious, incandescent feelings for Liena. Even with no hope for anything beyond friendship. He wondered that he'd ever become attached to Barbara, so cool did his feelings now seem. But then everything from that period of his life seemed cool. Everything before that bright morning in Valletta beneath the sun and the bombs and the screaming of the city.

He tried to write a poem, just for an exercise, but it kept turning into the most trite and sentimental rot, and he tore it up and burned the evidence.

Before he'd parted from Liena, Edmund fixed another evening to meet her. She didn't exactly resist, neither did she seem enthusiastic. It lifted his heart while ripping it. He already knew this was not a relationship. He was merely a moth to her candle, but that was OK. Any time he got to spend in her presence was alright by him. He had never met anyone like her. Knew he never would again, even if he survived long enough to make never a meaningful span.

The bombers came early that evening, barely before darkness had fallen, coming out of the gloom of the east. It caught the people of Valletta out, and far more of them were out in the open than last time. For the first time, Edmund sensed a little panic in Liena as she rushed round with the other ARP wardens, shepherding people – civilians, military, government bureaucrats, whoever – into the shelters. Because of the rush, some filled quicker than others, and a press began to form on the streets around the entrances.

The two of them resorted to dashing around the accreting crowds, pleading with them to go elsewhere.

"There's another shelter just two...no, three streets away," Edmund panted. "On..." He tried to remember the name of the street. This family was Maltese, and all the streets had two names.

The mother – she was perhaps five years older than Liena, but her three boys of various ages, her matronly demeanour, made her seem another generation entirely – shrugged. "We live here. My daughter is down there. She will be expecting us."

The first bombers were overhead now. Edmund watched, mesmerised as dashes of light, glowing ellipses on a black page, drifted upwards into the sky. Bursts of orange, instantaneous carnations, punctuated the heavens.

The family was still standing in line. "You're queuing!" Edmund spluttered, unforgivably. "The bombers are here and you're... Filing. Like...like you're going to a funeral."

The woman shrugged. "We will be. For somebody here. Soon."

He felt a hand on his elbow. Liena. "There's nothing more you can do," she said. "Come away. There may be others we can persuade."

When they had finally reached a shelter themselves, they sat, exhausted, backs against the frigid stone wall. Edmund felt a subtle weight, like a bird landing, on his shoulder. Liena had laid her head on it. It was only for a moment. He would always remember that weight, the delicacy of it. He tried to put his arm around her shoulder, but she shrugged it off.

"I don't know what you're looking for, Edmund," Liena said, voice suddenly tired, "but I don't think you'll find it with me. If you want a friend. Someone to talk to who isn't a boy. Then alright. You can see me now and again. As to anything else, you can forget it. I may be unmarriageable but I'm still a good Catholic."

"Who says you're unmarriageable?" Edmund said, and no sooner had the words sounded out than he wished they hadn't.

Liena did not laugh, as he suspected she might, but simply shook her head. Not unkindly. Pityingly, perhaps, as she met his gaze. "Lieutenant. Are you going to propose and take me away from all this?"

Edmund felt the heat in his cheeks burning even over the scorching Malta air. He muttered something about that not being what he meant. Wasn't it, though? Not even slightly? Was there hidden in the words some ludicrous idea of bringing back to England a lean, hard Maltese woman who had endured things to make most English girls run screaming, who could silence with a stare and yet still enchant with a smile? Wasn't she a kind of rock you could anchor your life to and fear nothing thereafter? Idiot.

"You're very strange for an English boy," she said, looking at him for what felt like the first time. "Anyway, it's impossible. You're not a Catholic."

When he got back to Hal Far in the morning, there were half a dozen new craters in the runway, and Godden had returned. Edmund marvelled. In the few days he had been gone, he had receded in Edmund's consciousness as though looked at through the wrong end of a telescope. And now the telescope had been turned around the right way.

"Thought any more about my Ramrod mission?" Godden asked him as they walked out to the Hurricanes to wait at readiness for a call.

He shrugged. "It's just as much of a lousy idea as it was last week."

"Ha!" Godden grinned, showing his teeth. "No imagination. That's your trouble. You've been too long in the system. Some Commander Flying telling you when to get in and out of your kite, when to take off, land, fight, withdraw. Telling you when you eat, sleep and shit. You need to use this a bit more, Clyde old chum," he said, tapping Edmund sharply on the top of his skull. "Or at least devote a bit more of it to fighting and a bit less to French poetry. Seen any more imaginary Jerries?"

"No Jerries of any kind, thanks."

"Pity. Anyway, I'd have thought getting shot up by a single kite would persuade you of the benefits of a sweep over enemy territory. Winds them up. Reminds them they're not invulnerable. Maybe even makes 'em hold back some of their fighters in case we hit 'em again."

Edmund could hardly disagree, but since Operation 'Harpoon' had barely added any petrol to the island's dwindling stocks, he imagined there was precious little scope for offensive missions.

Godden was itching to get back into the air and was first up, but as luck would have it, *Faithless* developed a fault when the engine was warming up, so Edmund took the first call, propelled into the air seemingly only partly by the Rolls-Royce Merlin and partly by the sheer force of Godden's frustration.

"Hello Gondar," he radioed when he'd climbed and reduced to cruising speed. "This is Exile Two, taking over Exile Flight. Exile One is U/S. What's my vector?" and feeling far too much satisfaction when Gondar rasped "Hello Exile Leader, Exile Leader," to give him the course.

A Hudson on the flight from North Africa reported a man in the sea. No dinghy, no fluoroscene dye. It was a needle in a mountain of hay. With Godden's comments about his eyesight ringing in his ears, Edmund headed out on the course the controller had given him with trepidation.

He spotted the little chevron of white in the blue immensity that marked the launch easily this time – funny how quickly the eyes adjusted – and called it in. "Seagull Zero Seven, this is Exile Leader, I see you. I'll be overhead in a moment."

"Hello Exile Leader, Seagull Zero Seven confirming. Good to hear your voice Clyde."

"You too, Patchy."

"No God today?"

"His kite had a snag."

"The Lord moves in mysterious ways. Pity, could have done with his eyes."

Edmund smiled. Godden's bloody eyes again. Shame he couldn't look where he was going on the ground.

They reached the position given by the Hudson and began their search. With only one Hurricane, Edmund had to keep an eye out for fighters too. It was surely impossible. And a man, in the water, on his own for hours. The chances he was still alive were minimal.

But there was still a chance. He slid back the canopy and started searching.

When HSL 107 was well into her second square search, Edmund checked his fuel. Still plenty for the moment, but there would reach a point where he would have to make a choice. Stay on station and keep searching - but taking the chance that there would be no enemy aircraft. A dogfight in that state would mean too little petrol to get home...

Edmund passed that boundary with barely a thought. His fuel continued to run down. He was flying along the lines of the waves, looking along the troughs, hoping to see the crests breaking around something.

If there was a man down there, he would see him, damn it! From this height, with this visibility. He just needed to fly over them. He must be down there somewhere...so it was a case of simply being thorough. He began another pattern starting from the initially given position, adjusted with a hurried mental arithmetic for wind drift.

And just as staring at nothing but empty expanse had become mesmeric, there was something down there. But damn, it was not a man, just debris.

Debris from an aircraft. It was obvious. There was a bit of wing. And that was petrol on the surface of the water. You could see when the light reflected on it how it smoothed out the ripples.

Edmund took a guess that any occupant would be downwind. A parachute would have drifted...well...he made another calculation - and turned the Hurricane round.

He had enough fuel, as long as he could stay at cruise. Maybe he could get to one of the other airfields if he couldn't quite reach Hal Far. He pushed such thoughts out of his mind. He needed all his faculties for searching.

And there, as simple as that, was a man. Edmund saw him so clearly it was a wonder he had not found him an hour ago. A body, he reminded himself, probably a body. It was unusual though. The lifejacket was white, maybe pale buff, not the yellow Mae West pilots mostly wore.

And then the body waved at him.

He called it in to the HSL, voice shaking and circled, tightly, determined not to lose the fellow now. The boat arrived in a sluice of white foam, and in moments the crew had a man in the water, helping to hoist the airman onto the deck.

"Well done Exile Leader," Patchy crackled over the VHF. "One very happy Eyetie here. He says to thank you."

"He's very welcome," Edmund replied, thinking of the Macchi pilot who let him go the other day, his heart soaring a thousand feet above the Hurricane. A life saved. A life. "Very welcome indeed."

"You wasted all that time, and petrol, and barely got *Hopeless* back here, and all for a bloody Eyetie?" Godden stormed when Edmund made his report. "Don't do it again."

"We didn't know it was an Eyetie before we picked him up," Edmund protested. "The report just said there was a pilot in the water."

Godden rolled his eyes. "You must have seen he wasn't in British kit. Even you could have told that."

"Well, yes. But only once we'd found him. Would you have just left him there?"

"No. I'd have machine-gunned the bastard."

"Godden!" Edmund's mouth was hanging open. He shut it.

"Oh, don't be such a bloody prig," Godden snapped. "They do it to us. Anyway, of course I wouldn't shoot a man in the water, what do you think I am?"

"Of course, sorry Godden." Whatever you say...

"I should think so too. Alright, finish your paperwork and go and get changed. I dare say you've got a date with your old Maltese crone later."

"I beg your..."

"Stow it, Clyde. Get lost. You're on with me again tomorrow morning so make sure you're back in time and fresh, okay?"

As it happened, he did not have a date – Godden clearly didn't know everything around here, even if he knew far more than seemed decent. In fact, there wasn't much to do so he found a shady spot with a good view of the airfield and, while jotting down a few lines in the service of his stuttering poetry career, half-watched the activity. Soldiers from the nearby service unit were out, filling in the new holes. A squadron of Spits at readiness sat and waited for half an hour, then took off in a blizzard of dust. A couple of Stringbags left with depth charges under the wings. A Baltimore flew in and left ten minutes later. And then there must have been a call-out, as he saw *Faithless* and *Uncharitable* taxiing out. He watched the Hurricanes' progress – Godden heading straight, almost fast enough to lift the tail, Cocke slower, weaving deliberately.

Edmund jumped to his feet. Godden was steering right towards a repair party. He'd surely turn aside...but the Hurricane kept going, propeller slashing at the air...the pongoes had noticed, were leaping away, running in all directions. Edmund breathed. At least the men were out of the way, but Godden was still heading towards a partially filled crater.

But the pilot must have seen the soldiers fleeing from out under the Hurri's nose and dropped the throttle, standing on the brakes so hard the tail hopped off the ground and the prop blades missed the dirt by inches. Edmund exhaled. Thank heaven! What the hell was he playing at?

The two Hurris sorted themselves out and departed. The airfield quietened a little and after quarter of an hour, Edmund rose to retreat to his quarters when he heard an engine. A Merlin, unmistakably. Were the Spits coming back?

No, it was a Hurri. A problem with one of the kites? Please God they hadn't been bounced... There didn't seem to be anything wrong with it, as it joined the circuit and began to curve round into wind to land. No smoke or trail of coolant. It landed a little hesitantly. It was Cocke. He could tell from the way the machine moved. Careful, none of the brashness of Godden's handling. Amazing what you could see when you knew what you were looking for.

Edmund began packing up and went back into barrack block he called home. He realised as he did so how tired he was. He hadn't had more than a couple of hours sleep after the air raid on Valletta, and sitting in the sun had drained him. He lay on his bed and immediately fell asleep.

...And woke, with no sense of how much time might have passed. He must've flaked out so quickly he'd left the door ajar. He could hear voices from down the corridor. Not knowing quite why, he pulled himself to his feet and followed the sound.

As he walked along the corridor, the voices echoed louder along the cinderblock tunnel. Then there was only one voice. Raised. Sounded like Godden. The sound was coming from Cocke's room. The door was open. Edmund peered round it, in time to see – bloody hell! – Godden stepping forward and grasping Cocke by the lapels. For a second Edmund froze to the spot, just outside the doorway. Should he intervene?

"You little shit," Godden hissed. "You fucking little coward. I know what's up with you, and if you leave me on my tod again with the sky full of bloody Macchis I will tear off your skin and wear it like pyjamas."

"Sorry Godden!" Cocke stammered, face like whitewash. "It was the kite, it's defective, it's-"

Godden leaned right into Cocke's face. "The only thing defective around here is your fucking backbone."

Cocke sniffed. "Your Hurri went U/S yesterday-" but Godden silenced him with a glare. Edmund could not see if Cocke was crying, but it sounded like it. He knew he should stop this, he-

"You need to put this right, don't you?" Godden's voice was soft now. Pure menace.

Cocke nodded.

"You need to put this and all the other little incidents, right, right? French, and Mills, and Moore, and Tomlinson and the others?"

Cocke started to sob at that. Edmund cleared his throat. Both of them stared at him. Godden released Cocke's lapels and stormed out, glaring at Edmund as he passed.

Cocke straightened his jacket, stepped towards Edmund, and closed the door.

Edmund, mind spinning with what he had just seen, retreated to his quarters and lay on the bed. Was Godden really victimising Cocke for the state of his aircraft? The Hurricanes were old, used far beyond their expected life, and each of them might fail at any time. That said, Cocke did seem to be suffering the lion's share of the snags. That in itself wasn't too surprising. Sometimes you just seemed to get a duff kite. A 'rogue', some people called them. But then he reminded himself that Cocke had been flying different aircraft when he'd suffered the last two scares.

Maybe he was just over-cautious with the readouts.

But what were the 'incidents' that Godden had mentioned? And who were the people he'd named?

There was more going on here than Edmund knew about. But what could he do about it? What should he? Cocke would be going home soon, out of this, away from Godden. Would it be soon enough?

***

Edmund tried to push the unpleasant business out of his mind. He had missions to fly. And there was Liena. On Thursday afternoon she finally met him for something other than helping her with her ARP rounds. He borrowed a car from an RAF pilot – hired, really, for an exorbitant sum for petrol – collected Liena from Hamrun, where she'd got the bus, and they drove out to the island's west coast. Liena directed him down a track off the coast road, and presently to stop. There stood the ruins of an ancient temple, the religion that had led to its construction now utterly lost in an ocean of time, while the stones remained, resisting the violence of the sun, the winds from the sea, the stupid destructiveness of man. They walked down the rounded flank of the hillside, until they could see a square tower looking out over the depthless sea. It looked ancient, like something out of the Iliad, but Liena told him it was not old, just a few hundred years. They sat on a blanket on the ground, and once again Liena laid her head softly on his shoulder. The gentle pressure of her, the warmth, the power she held so lightly. The sea twinkled in the sun. Edmund begged to her God to let the moment last forever.

God had other ideas. "I have to get back," she said, almost in a whisper, and then, soft as a whisper he felt her lips brush his cheek. He turned in surprise but she was already walking away. They drove back to the city in a beautiful torment of silence.

"When can I see you next?" he asked hotly as she climbed out of the car.

"I don't know," Liena replied, avoiding his gaze. "I will be busy."

And she was gone.

Edmund returned to Hal Far in quiet anguish. The worst was forgotten when he saw that on his bed there was a letter. For him! It was from Vickery, the journalist! Posted from Gib. He scanned down it. Oh, it was good to hear from the old man. He'd responded to Edmund's words about Cocke and his painting with an interesting suggestion.

"You may have heard about the War Artists' Advisory Committee. They look out for artists who can provide an artistic record of the war. Might be something for your chum to consider? Sounds as though he's already well on his way. I know a fellow on the committee who can put a word in, if you could get me a couple of examples of his work."

And right at the end, a line that jumped off the paper at him. "Glad to hear you're writing some poetry, I rather hoped you might, and sorry to hear you are struggling. If I might offer a word of advice, unlooked for I know, perhaps put aside the poetry you want to write, and focus on the poetry you have to write."

Thoughts of sparkling seas and ruminations on life fled. Malta spiralled through Edmund's mind. The people. The air-raids. The quiet tenacity.

He picked up a pen and wrote, and wrote, and wrote.

A Burial

Our burial is yet inverted. We are interred in
Air, in Sound, in limestone, breathe
Machine-voice keens.
The buried and the mourners mingled
Still by bone of fractured streetwall, mouths
Of open roofs. The mourners queue and wait
Outside, and none know who they mourn.

In air as time, the threads of futures
Meet. The wings that bring the bombs,
The bombs that sort the order of

The mourning.
We are interred in air, In fear, inevitable
As gravity. The Earth unseals, invites,
And all shall join the dead to come
Within, until they know who's turn.

***

Edmund wrote to Liena, care of the ARP HQ in Hamrun. It was only a couple of lines. Tepid pleasantries, a forwarding address if she cared to contact him. It was a last act of desperation. He left out everything that he wanted to say. That he would throw himself at her feet. Beg to know what he had done wrong. Plead for just one more moment in her presence. Every day that went by without a reply drove the spike of rusting steel a little further into his heart.

At least there was flying. Sunday, he flew in the morning with Godden and the afternoon with Cocke. The morning was tense. A fruitless search for a Spitfire pilot who'd gone in after a big dogfight, and several times Gondar warned them that a large plot was heading in their direction, only to turn away before reaching them.

The afternoon was worse. A sky full of pilots and a twitchy Cocke.

"I think the oil pressure's going again. Honestly, this bloody engine. Kite needs a new one."

"Just hang on, it's fine."

"Alright, but to be honest the temps aren't great either."

"Hang on." Edmund took him through some throttle and mixture settings that ought to bring things back to reasonable levels.

"Hello Exile Flight, this is Gondar, bogeys inbound north west of you, angels ten, watch out for 'em."

"Understood Gondar. OK Exile Two, you keep an eye out for the dinghy, I'll watch out for the fighters."

To Cocke's credit, he did as he was told, despite the occasional gripe about his engine. And then the fighters came, carving down out of the sun, streams of tracer flickering out, ephemeral grasping claws. "Stay on me," he puffed to Cocke as he manoeuvred this way and that, chess-moving to prevent the fighters getting between the Hurricanes and Malta. "Stay on me," as a black, snub-nosed fighter dropped in behind, barrel rolling to dump speed, as he pulled into a tight turn, "stay on me," as he rolled inverted, pulled back on the stick, watched the sea encompass everything, scroll down through the windscreen to rush past a mere fifty or sixty feet below, finally the sky reappearing above.

The manoeuvre had peeled away the fighter that had been trying to latch onto his tail. He watched it, a few hundred feet above and too far away to catch him without a long stern-chase. But Cocke had disappeared too. Muttering curses, Edmund searched the sky. He tried to raise Cocke on the VHF. And then he called control. "Gondar, do you have a fix on Exile Two?"

"Hello Exile Leader, no. Will keep trying to raise him."

When Edmund landed at Hal Far he experienced intense relief, puzzlement and fury to see *Uncharitable* sitting on the apron, having arrived ten minutes previously, according to his fitter, Mike.

"What the bloody hell happened to him," Edmund snapped, jutting his chin at the innocent Hurricane.

"Oh. Said he lost you when the Eyeties came down, sir. Flew about looking for you but the sky was empty and his coolant temp was getting a bit high so he came back."

Edmund exhaled raggedly. "Mike, I wondered if I might have a word."

"Aye sir, what is it?" A look of concern flickered on the seaman mechanic's face, replaced with pure professionalism. "Nothing wrong with *Hopeless* I hope?"

"It's not about my aeroplane. She's just the ticket." As much as a machine of her age and wear could possibly be, anyway.

"Oh, thank you sir."

"You're welcome. It's about... Sub-Lieutenant Cocke's aeroplane, actually."

Mike's expression immediately hardened. "I shouldn't sir. Was there anything about your machine?"

Edmund rubbed his eyes. "I know I'm asking a lot. Too much, of course, and you've served with him for months and I've just got here."

"That's right, sir. And his rigger and fitter." Mike's voice was full of wariness and disappointment. An officer might easily put him in an impossible position, Edmund realised.

"I wouldn't even mention it, but it might be putting people at risk. There've been several times when the Sub-Lieutenant felt his machine was going U/S. As it was, it was alright – we didn't have to abort any sorties or abandon any ditched crews – but it seems to be happening a little too often for comfort."

Mike shuffled his feet. "Ah. Is that right, sir? Hmm. Yes. Well, you'd have to speak to Mr Cocke really."

He recalled the exchange between Cocke and Godden with a jolt. Godden grasping Cocke's jacket, shouting in his face... "I've listened to Sub Le'tenant Cocke's thoughts on the subject."

"Ah. Yes. Well. His rigger and fitter are good men, sir. Just one of those things, maybe."

"It's just that Cocke's Hurricane always seems to go U/S when we're in the presence of the enemy. Why do you think that might be?"

Mike looked at him sharply, looked away, back again, away. He closed his eyes, pursed his lips. Edmund wanted to tell him it was alright, not to bother, apologise. But it was important. There was something not right here.

"Has there been anything wrong with it, when it gets back here?"

"I really can't say, sir."

"It's important. Not just for me, you understand. Or Godden, even. But Cocke himself. Damn it, I like the fellow, and I think he's reached the end of his tether and deserves to go home. I don't think it's doing anyone any good him still being here. Am I wrong?"

"Alright, I'll tell you," Mike breathed. "But only to help Mister Cocke, okay?"

"Of course. That's the only reason I'm asking."

"Now pardon my saying so sir, but of you please, you won't repeat a word of this to anyone, and if anyone says anything to you, this didn't come from me, right?"

Edmund nodded, effected to look kindly.

"Well he started to get a touch of the Twitch. Malta Twitch, they call it. Not the end of the world, lots of pilots get it. The quacks ain't sure what causes it. Exhaustion, stress, too many bouts of Malta Dog, maybe lots of things. People start to get a twitch. Like muscles, just moving without you meaning to."

"Cocke's hand?"

"Exactly. But that's not the main thing. That's just a symptom. It's like a progressive..." Mike was sweating now, and Edmund suspected it had little to do with the beating sun.

"Go on."

Mike went on, voice below a mutter. This had been building for a while, and Edmund realised the mechanic had given it a fair bit of thought. "A progressive...loss of nerve. Pilots start thinking there's something wrong with the plane. Some people think it's just cowardice, but I reckon it's like...what do you call it? A defence mechanism. That's it. When you're that wound up, your brain starts finding little things to worry about. Sounds that you think are the engine going rough. You think you see the instruments moving funny. Or you get convinced the instruments are wrong."

It made sense. There was so much to keep an eye on in an aeroplane, so much that could go wrong and kill you. The range of parameters, varying according to conditions. It was tough at the best of times. When you started getting paranoid that anything might be going wrong... Edmund nodded for Mike to continue.

"It didn't come from nowhere, you see. There was one time Mister Cocke's Albacore had an engine failure on take-off. Thing just seized with no warning when he was just airborne. They went off the end of the cliff into the sea. No-one was hurt, but I think it shook him."

"So, what happened?"

Mike looked left and right, then over his shoulder. Even though no-one was around.

"When that starts working away at you, it's like a drive. An *imperative*. To turn back. You can't help feel that something's badly wrong. He started turned back on a few missions. Snags with his kite that turned out to be nothing much. Not enough really to worry the CO. Happens to a lot of people after a while. Most get over it and get a hold of themselves. Anyway, about a month ago the squadron went on a night raid to Catania, to torpedo ships in the harbour. Four Albacores. Cocke was tail-end charlie. He started to think his machine had engine trouble. The way he told it the thing was on the point of blowing up. So he turned back, but because they were on radio silence, he couldn't tell the flight leader. In the dark, the third aircraft didn't realise he'd left the formation. So, a bit later when one of the

TAGs spotted the exhaust glow of another aircraft a bit behind, it didn't bother them."

"Oh Christ. Night fighter?"

"Yeah. Blew two of them out of the sky and the leader's machine was barely able to make it back."

"And Cocke's engine?"

"Running perfectly."

"Hmm."

"Well nothing happened, officially at least. No-one could prove what happened. But everyone could see what'd happened to Mr Cocke. Eaten up by guilt, he was. And if you ask me..."

He mimed tipping a flask into his mouth. That made sense. The scent of booze hanging around him at odd times. More than anyone else, anyway.

"Commander Haynes took him off flying for a bit," Mike went on, "but he was determined to get back on, even though he's getting near the end of his tour. Almost hysterical, he was. So, when we got the Hurris for ASR, Commander Haynes let Mr Cocke fly one. But he wants to be back on ops. Before his tour runs out. I think if he could fly one operation and not get the wind up, he'd be happy."

"How was he on Albacores? Before the Twitch?"

"Pretty good, if you ask me sir. Before the Twitch, that is. Completely different job flying fighters to TBRs. Some fellows take to it, others don't."

"Yes, quite." It was usual for pilots finishing near the top of their course to be assigned to fighters, those with less good scores to TBRs. Which was not to say that they were worse pilots for the job they were doing, necessarily, and really it took different skills to fly a torpedo kite. Edmund wasn't sure he could manage it. But there was something about the twitchiness of a fighter – particularly a Hurricane – the speed with which things happened, that some pilots never quite got on top of.

Particularly if they were starting to get muscle twitches and their reactions getting poor. And they were self-medicating with ever greater quantities of alcohol.

Edmund nodded slowly. "Perhaps putting Cocke in a Hurricane was the worst things Haynes could have done."

"That's not for me to say, sir."

"No, no. I understand. Thank you, Mike. I won't breathe a word, don't worry. Oh, but there is one more thing."

"Sir?"

"It's not a question. I'm just going to offer an opinion. If you want to confirm or deny, that's up to you. Sub-Lieutenant Godden. His eyesight is remarkable at long distances but dreadful closer up, yes?"

The expression on Mike's face told Edmund all he needed to know.

As he walked back to the station buildings, he caught sight of a sprinting figure. It stopped, raised an arm and struck out in his direction. It was Godden. He panted and grinned. "Hugh-Pugh's given his blessing to our show. We're hitting Gela. It's set for next Tuesday at dawn. Haynes'll ask for volunteers but you're already pencilled in. Now we need to practice." And he ran off towards the CO's office.

It was only when he filled in his combat report that Edmund thought about the fighters he'd dodged. Small wings with rounded, almost pointed tips. A heavyset nose capped with a big rounded spinner. They were Messerschmitts, not Macchis. The Luftwaffe was back. And that threw an entirely different light on a mission into the hornets' nest.

Week 3

30 June 1942

Gela was a fighter station near the south coast of Sicily. It was home to at least three fighter squadrons - and bristled with flak guns. And then there was Edmund's suspicion that the Germans had returned. Attacking with three clapped-out Hurricanes was suicide. Haynes had indeed asked for volunteers. Edmund did not put his name forward. Godden tracked him down, insisting he volunteer. Edmund refused.

Godden had not taken no for an answer the first time, or the second. On the third, he exploded, told Edmund he'd be glad when he'd ponced off back to the sea and he hoped he'd get torpedoed in the night. With a plummeting feeling in his stomach, Edmund heard that Cocke had volunteered. *Why the hell did he go and do that?* Edmund wondered. But in his heart he already knew.

It was only right that Edmund told Cocke that he wasn't taking part. He'd find out sooner or later, and he didn't want him to hear it from Godden. He caught up with the other pilot in the crew room. Cocke was getting into his flying gear. He grinned tightly when he saw Edmund, which made the corner of his eye flicker.

"Low-level practice flight. Aren't you coming? You'd better get ready." Cocke fished in his pocket and brought out a cigarette. His hand was shaking so much as he lit it, he could barely hold the matchbox. His palms looked clammy.

"It'll be good to fly on this show with you, Clyde," Cocke said when he had taken a couple of puffs, though his breathing barely seemed to have calmed. "I like the idea of going into that cauldron with a friend by my side. A real friend."

Edmund's mouth twisted awkwardly. "You hadn't heard then? Well I wanted to tell you myself. I'm not coming."

Cocke's smile faded. His eyes were narrow then wide, disbelieving, accusing. "I don't understand. You're one of us. How can you not be coming? Has your squadron recalled you? Why?"

He had not imagined it would be this difficult. "It's because I don't agree with it. I don't think it's a good use of the aircraft. Or the men."

Cocke was still staring, still not understanding.

"It's too risky," Edmund went on. "We could lose all three Hurris, all three pilots, and not achieve anything at all."

"But...but you're one of us now."

"I know. But I can't do this."

"What does your opinion on the mission have to do with it?" Cocke balanced the Cape to Cairo in the recess of the ashtray with some effort, and folded his arms. "We have a job to do."

Edmund shrugged. "I'm doing a job, thank you very much."

"No, no. I mean the main job." Cocke clenched his fists and shifted from foot to foot. "Winning. Don't you think we have to do everything we can? Otherwise, what would happen to the world?"

This was ridiculous. When had Cocke started thinking like this? Godden. Damn Godden for getting into his head this way. Well, maybe Edmund could persuade him too. "I'm helping us win too, you know. ASR is important. As important to the war as anything. Look at me, I'm just one pilot. The other day I helped pull a pilot out of the drink. Another two a couple of days before that." They were Macleod's words coming out of Edmund's mouth, but it didn't make them any less true. "When I got here, I promised not to let a single aircrewman go if it was in my power to save them. And this is putting them at risk, isn't it? If we lose the aircraft, the pilots, how will we co-operate with the boats? They'll be on their own again."

"But sooner or later, we have to be prepared to throw our weight into the scale. All of us, individually. Our lives. Nothing less will do. We have to. We *need* to. Or what's it for? If everyone thought like you, we'd never find anyone to go up and shoot down the bombers."

If everyone thought like me, they'd never find anyone to fly those bloody bombers every blasted day, Edmund thought. He kept it to himself. What happened if those idiots found themselves shot down in the sea on their little sortie, anyway? It would be up to him and the launch to make sure they didn't drown.

"It's alright to be afraid of dying," Cocke said. Edmund stared at him, but Cocke was looking through him as if he wasn't there at all. "Sometimes I think you can only live by dying and being remembered. It was a poet who said that, I think. Do you know who by any chance? No, I don't suppose." He lit a Cape to Cairo in his characteristic way, like starting a Hurricane from cold. Edmund waited.

"Dying," Cocke went on, talking to the universe, to his cigarette, to the sky. "It's the hardest thing of all. When I'm sitting there in the cockpit, it's as if I'm composed of a sort of vivid energy, burning out into the world, and preserving that energy is the most important thing. Down here it seems ridiculous. I suppose I'm just a coward."

If that's the only way you live, Edmund thought, the idea circling and repeating, then I never will.

"Viv. You're not a coward," he said. "No more than any of us. There's a difference between being scared of dying and not seeing any point in it. Look..." He tightened his fists. Tried again. "Look, I know a chap who you can talk to. There's a sort of commission of war artists that I've heard of. Have you heard of that? We could try to get you a role with them. I'm sure once they see your work they'll be delighted to have you."

Cocke's eyes widened, and what remained of the colour in his lips fled. "No! God, no! The thought of painting as...as a way to get out of my responsibilities! Why would you say such a thing?"

"That's not what I meant." Edmund had raised his palms, warding off the accusation. "I don't mean that at all. It would be a way to use your ability. To make a difference. To help with the war."

"No," Cocke shouted. "Why would you try to tempt me this way? Don't you understand? It has to be in the air."

"What does, Viv? What has to be in the air?"

"My reckoning. My..." His eyes widened. "My *penance*. Godden says-"

"Good grief," Edmund spat. "You think that's all your life is for?" He turned his back, took a few steps towards the door, turned back. "Listen, a few days ago I was in Valletta during an air raid. I went into a shelter with some civilians. And they sat there waiting. Patient. Trusting. Resigned... No, not resigned, accepting...whatever might happen. It was the bravest thing I ever saw. Not that their lives might end. But that they might end *or go on*. Every day they have to find the courage to go back to their ordinary humdrum lives after almost being blown apart. They don't run outside in the street every time the bombers come over just to prove themselves."

"You're...you're turning aside in the face of the enemy." It wasn't just Cocke's hand that was shaking now. His whole body seemed to vibrate. "*You're* the coward! Get out. Get out of here. GET OUT."

Edmund rushed out without looking back. He had to find Godden. He scoured the base and found him in the officers' mess.

"I need to have a word with you about Cocke," he panted. "About this Ramrod mission of yours."

"Oh yes, Clyde?" The other pilot put his hands in his pockets and said nothing more.

"Well. I've just spoken to him. I don't think he's...in the right sort of state."

"I don't know what you mean, old chum."

Edmund huffed. "You can't think he's fit to fly it, can you?"

Godden looked at him levelly for several seconds, betraying nothing. "Are you looking to deprive me of yet another pilot for my show?" he said eventually. "Is that how you plan to stop it?"

Godden's pride. Everything was about his pride. Good God, it could cost lives! He tried to adopt a reasonable tone. It sounded wheedling in his ears. "Godden, think, man. See sense. You know he's not right for it. He'll get to go home soon and put this place behind him. Find someone else."

"Skipper asked for three volunteers," Godden replied, eyes narrowed. "And three volunteers he got. Anyway, have you spoken to Viv? He's quite happy about it." He stepped forward, putting his face right in Edmund's. "Keen as mustard in fact. So I suppose that's that," he finished, tapping Edmund on the chest with each syllable.

"You've poisoned his mind, you bloody madman!" Edmund exploded, snapping his mouth shut before he could make it worse. He stared at Godden, jaw clamped so tight it took a deliberate effort to continue without screaming. "He's determined to prove he's not a coward or die in the attempt." Godden wouldn't turn his gaze away. He was winning. Edmund pushed once more. "I think he believes that to prove he's not a coward, he *has* to die in the attempt. You brought him to this, it's up to you to bring him back."

"Don't you understand?" Godden smiled. There was a savage gleam in his eye. "Cocke wants this! He wants to go out in a blaze of glory. You've seen him. He's destroyed. Hollow. There's nothing of him left. Do you want to send that back to his parents? You think the Empire needs the likes of him wandering round telling everyone how dreadful this ghastly war is?"

Edmund flinched. "Good God. You actually want him to die?"

Godden did not speak. His silence and his expression said everything.

Edmund inhaled sharply. This was senseless! Delirium! He'd rather Cocke was killed than let on to anyone that his nerve had gone? He almost shrieked "Christ, Godden. He's mentally and physically exhausted. Done in. He deserves to go home. Pick up whatever of his life that he can. None of us are who we used to be - but come on. Given a bit of time, he could get better."

"There's nothing left of him to get better. You didn't know him before. He was different."

"That's a bit strong, isn't it? This is war. It hits everyone. Doesn't he deserve the chance to find a bit of peace?"

Godden snorted. "He deserves that, does he? Deserves that more than the people he failed? They won't get the chance, though, will they? They're spread all over the Sicilian Channel!"

Edmund stiffened. "The night raid? When Cocke turned back? That's what this is all about?"

Godden raised an eyebrow. "Someone's been talking. That won't do. Loose lips sink ships. Which is more than anyone can say for Mister Cocke. We lost good people that night. Better than him."

Edmund shook his head. It all made sense. But this was going to end in someone getting killed. "It was a tragedy, I know," he said, hands out in placation. "Stupid, senseless. But Cocke's been punishing himself ever since. You can't do worse to him than he's done to himself."

"Maybe I can't," he said, brimming with scorn. "I do like a challenge though."

"Jesus, Godden. His tour ends soon and he'll be out of your life for good."

"Why should someone like that get to go home when better people didn't? What's he got to offer the world?"

"His painting, for a start," Edmund barked. He fought to soften his voice. "He has a talent. You've seen his stuff. It says more about the war here than I ever could. Maybe it'll help people understand what men like you have been through."

There was a mix of triumph and viciousness written across Godden's face. "Have you looked at any of those paintings lately? I suggest you pay a bit closer attention, and then tell me if you think Cocke's work is fit to be seen by the public. Or anyone without a particularly strong stomach."

Edmund backed away. What was Godden talking about? He'd seen those paintings himself. Godden laughed. "You haven't seen his newest work, have you? Go on, why don't you take a shufti?" As Edmund ran out of the mess, Godden's voice chased him, "*I'd burn the lot if I were you! For the sake of his poor family!*"

He ran straight to Cocke's quarters. They were empty, of course. Cocke was in the crew room. The painting of the launch was still on the easel. There was more of it now. A dinghy beside the HSL. The whole thing had more detail added from the last time he had seen it. It felt like an eye focussing. Edmund peered more closely. The airman in the dinghy was a corpse. Even with the small size of the painting it was obvious. It was virtually a skeleton, a bleached-white skull-grin greeting the rescuers, only a few shreds of flesh and clothing adhering to the bones.

That was gruesome, but only reflected the ghastly truth of what ASR could sometimes mean.

And then he looked at all the other figures crewing the launch. They were corpses too. The same skeletal features. The same shredded flesh and clothes. A slow tumbling started in Edmund's gut, as if his body were being sucked inside out. He went to the wardrobe, ripped aside the sheet that was draped over the canvases. The painting of the dockers unloading the ship was uppermost, and he was about to move it aside when he noticed it was not the same as when he had last looked at it. The faces of everyone in the scene were dead. Grinning skulls, catastrophic wounds, burned and broken flesh. He flipped to the picture of the air-raid shelter. The faces were no longer calm and resilient, they were screaming in pain and terror. The soldiers repairing the runway were on fire. On every single painting, every single figure was dead, dying or facing an imminent, violent end. Edmund dropped the painting, slammed the wardrobe shut, and backed away from it, to the door, and away.

He had to find Haynes. Find him and stop Godden. The man was twisted. He'd kill everyone around him.

Haynes was in his office. Edmund barged past the secretary and stood in front of the squadron commander's desk. The Australian stared at him, eyes wide, but said nothing. *He allows it from Godden*, Edmund thought, *he can bloody well put up with it from me*.

He cleared his throat. "I wanted to have a word, sir. About Sub-Lieutenant Godden."

"Yes?"

"It's my opinion, sir, that he's dangerous."

"I know. And?"

Edmund's eyes widened. "I mean to say. That he...that I believe he poses a danger to his squadron mates."

Haynes sighed and leaned forward. "Listen, Lieutenant. I know damned well that Godden is a bloody menace. It's my job to make sure he's a bloody menace to the enemy as much as possible, and as little as possible to everyone around him. And that's what I'm doing."

"But sir, this plan to strafe Sicily-"

"It gives Godden something to focus his energies on so he's not destroying my aeroplanes and destabilising the squadron. And besides, it's a good plan. It might even work."

"And it might get everyone involved killed."

"By everyone, you mean Sub-Lieutenant Cocke."

"In all honesty, yes. He may be a decent TBR pilot but he can't handle a fighter, especially at low-level. And I believe he's burned out."

"Everyone here is burned out." Haynes threw up his arms. He was shouting. The secretary appeared at the door and Haynes shooed him away. "Everyone except you, and you didn't want to go. Cocke volunteered. It would be lovely if I had a queue of pilots to choose from, but I don't. Three Hurris. Three volunteers. Collins took the place that might have been yours. Cocke flies."

It was slipping away. But Edmund had promised himself.

No airman will be lost if it's in my power to save them.

And it was in his power to save Cocke. At least to save him from this mission, from Godden. The future was out of his hands.

He closed his eyes for a second. "I'll go."

"What?" Haynes craned his neck at Edmund as though he were trying to see in the dark.

"I'll go. I volunteer. Now you've got four volunteers and three Hurris. Scrub Cocke. I'll do it."

Haynes sighed, shook his head. "A minute ago you were saying what a terrible plan it was."

"It is. It's an unacceptable risk. But I choose to accept it."

The CO looked at him, a bird of prey sizing up a mouse, deciding whether it was worth diving for. "Alright," he said slowly. "Alright. You're on. But only if Godden agrees."

Godden did not.

"No," he said. "No, no, no. You had your chance. You made it perfectly clear what you think of this mission, and I can't trust that you'll pull your weight."

"Forget all that." Edmund did not look away from Godden's implacable gaze. He would not be forced down. "You know Cocke's low-level flying is piss-poor, and you know he doesn't have the reflexes for fighters, especially not at high speed on the bloody deck."

Godden smiled. "Be that as it may. It's my call."

"And it would be a sodding daft call to put Cocke in the kite when you could put me in it."

A smirk passed across Godden's face. "I think you let that almost-an-ace business go to your head, Clyde old pal. I've met many better pilots than you."

Edmund rolled his eyes. "And if any of them are available to you, put them on the mission. Look, forget all the personal stuff. You want this to succeed, yes? Then put the best pilots for the job onto it." Edmund had one card left to play. "And let's talk about eyesight for a moment, shall we? There might be certain people who could identify an individual speck of dust at ten miles but couldn't hit a barn door at point blank range because they can't even see it."

There was fury in Godden's eyes. His face was frozen. The colour had gone from it.

"Need to get in pretty close to bomb a hangar or a row of aeroplanes yes? Close enough that, hypothetically, someone who had eyesight like that, might struggle? Where someone with more common visual acuity might not? Hypothetically? Considering one of you can't fly at low-level and the other can't see at close quarters, it strikes me that you're loading a fair bit or responsibility onto poor old Collins."

Godden tipped his head back and looked at Edmund along his nose for some moments. "I'll think about it," he said, walking away.

And then stopped, turned. "Thought about it. No."

***

There was still a chance – half a chance, perhaps – that the mission would not go ahead. The next day, Edmund joined the party gathering to watch Godden make a few practice bomb runs on the parade ground. Perhaps the sheer idiocy of it would become so obvious, Haynes would call it off.

The Hurricane curved in at a mile's distance and began its run in. Even at a hundred feet the aircraft was clearly visible. "Plain as the nose on your face," Haynes muttered in disgust. He mimed holding a shotgun, and got off both imaginary barrels at his leisure before Godden had reached the airfield perimeter. "I'd like to be an AA gunner seeing that coming." Godden released the bombs, which arced lazily and thumped into the ground two hundred yards short of the target. Haynes growled. "No bloody good at all." Edmund's chest, which had been tighter and tighter, relaxed.

"Bit different from bombing in the Albacore, isn't it Godden?" Edmund sniped at the pilot as he stomped back to the party. He shot Edmund a filthy look but said nothing - and went into a huddle with Haynes to come up with an alternative approach. This time, he would pop up to fifteen hundred feet at a mile out and attack in a ten degree glide-bombing profile. It went smoothly – the bombs were only a hundred yards off and the Hurricane was going a lot faster when it approached, but was even more conspicuous on the run in. "No good. Bloody awful in fact. You'll be lucky to get one aircraft out of three as far as the target, and you still won't hit anything when you get there."

I could have bloody told you that, Edmund thought to himself but said nothing.

Godden tried again, popping up to a thousand feet half a mile away, but there was no time to stabilise the bomb run and the practice bombs went well wide of the target.

"Could we cross the coast further up and swing round to attack out of the sunrise?" someone asked when they had gathered for another conference.

Godden shook his head. "No chance, there's a blasted mountain range to the East."

"Do we have to take the bombs?" Collins suggested. "Could we not just come in on the deck and strafe?"

"With three-oh-threes? Bloody pop-guns. No, it needs to be bombs. They might not even bother to scramble otherwise."

"What about getting the Spits to go in first?"

"What would be the point of that? The point is to provoke their fighters into the air and hit them while they're still climbing."

"Five-thousand foot approach and steep dive bomb?"

"Still within ack-ack range on the approach. And the Hurri's not stressed for steep dive-bombing."

They argued over point after point but nothing was agreed. No option gave a good chance of hitting a target while not being hopelessly vulnerable to flak. Edmund watched the arguments going back and forth. He said nothing. If things continued like this, maybe the attack would be called off.

And then he had an idea.

It would work. It would be accurate. It would be as safe as anything else.

He waited. Perhaps someone else would come up with it.

"Christ, you're all hopeless," Godden spat. "This is a bloody war, you think you can get through it without facing a bit of flak?"

"It won't just be a bit," Haynes replied, making a visible effort to keep his voice level. "Gela's one of the most heavily defended places on Sicily. Maybe we could get Hugh-Pugh to change targets. Find an airfield we can approach from the East. Gerbini maybe."

"He won't change now. It took him this long to agree to it in the first place. And we've got to do it soon. If the Jerries *are* back," he said, glancing daggers at Edmund. "And Hugh-Pugh's off home soon, you know the fellow replacing him is an air-defence man, he mightn't go for something like this. It *has* to be now." He banged his hand on the table. "Has to be."

"It's your funeral," Haynes murmured.

Godden flashed an angry look at him. "You'd better order the flowers then."

It was going ahead. There was nothing anyone could do to stop it.

"Skip-bombing," Edmund said.

Everyone turned to look at him.

"Skip-bombing. Like the anti-ship boys do at sea, but it works on land too. Our squadron did a bit in the Western Desert. Stay low – thirty feet – and flat. Aim directly at the target. Release the bombs far enough away to pull up and miss any buildings. Takes balls of brass but it works."

"Bollocks. We'd knock our own tails off," Godden snapped.

Edmund shook his head. "The bombs bounce a bit, but not that much. Less on land than on water in fact – they only bounce up around ten feet or so. And because they don't hit nose first, the fuses don't trigger until they skip into something. Anyway, we can set them for a few seconds delay to be on the safe side.

Aim it right and you can plant them right through a hangar door. A dispersal pen. Anything."

Haynes scratched his head. "I can't see any reason why it wouldn't work. We should try it."

"Right." Godden grabbed his flying helmet.

"No." Haynes laid his hand on Godden's arm. "It was Clyde's suggestion. He can demo. Alright?"

Godden's brows clouded for a moment but then he nodded. "We'll all have to try it if it looks like it's going to work."

Edmund folded his arms, lifted his chin. "And if it works, I'm on the mission."

"Now look here-" Godden started, but Haynes held up his hand.

"Fair. He's the only one with any experience of this."

"Hey!" Cocke yelled, "whose spot does he take?"

"Okay," Edmund said, ignoring Cocke. He'd never tried it himself, only watched it. But the others didn't have to know that. "Just one request. As well as the cross, I could do with a couple of posts. I'll be low enough that a flat target will be hard to see. Space them...I dunno, seventy feet apart?"

The Hurricane's wingspan was 40 feet.

Haynes pushed his cap back. "We'll see to that. Go and prep your Hurri."

Hopeless was already having a pair of practice bombs fitted as he reached her. Tiny things that looked laughable, but they were designed to mimic the trajectory of a 250 lb bomb when dropped. He took off and circled the airfield, dipping down to take a look at the target area. A couple of maintainers were guying some posts up as he'd asked, and someone had had the bright idea of putting flags on them. Perfect.

He turned and flew back out to a couple of miles' distance, letting down to a hundred feet before reversing course, easing the Hurricane down to deck level and pushing up the speed to as near as possible to top – nudging 250 mph at this altitude. He felt the aircraft settle as if onto a cushion, the air trapped between the aircraft's wings and the ground.

The earth vanished under the Hurricane at a delirious pace, and the parade ground rushed up, a solid juggernaut. There, just to the right of the nose, were the flags! He tweaked the Hurricane's course with the rudder, merest dabs on the controls. Goodness, they were coming up quick. Not quite on target but good enough. He pickled the bombs at around five hundred feet distance, and hauled the Hurricane into a climbing left turn. His heart was pattering - and he heaved gulp after gulp of air into his lungs. As much of that was the compulsion to know if the skip-bombing had worked as adrenaline flooding his arteries from flying stupidly, dangerously low and fast. It would be like this on the raid itself, he realised. Little idea of what damage they'd done until they saw the recce photos afterwards. No chance to circle round and check the results. And that was if they made it back.

With a strange sense of calm, he landed, and taxied to *Hopeless*' revetment. A knot of people were gathered there. As he shut down the engine, he heard cheers and whistles.

Everyone was grinning. Even Godden, though his expression was somewhat fixed.

"That's the one! Just the ticket!" Haynes laughed, clapping him on the back. "Straight through the doors."

Godden picked a bit of debris off the sleeve of his jacket. He did not look up. "We all ought to try it. See that it wasn't a fluke."

Edmund smiled to himself. It was petty, but he enjoyed the moment anyway.

A guttural sound issued from Haynes. "You get one run each. That's all I can spare the petrol for."

Edmund stared at Godden and waited until the other pilot looked up. "I'm on the mission, then." It was not a question.

Godden scratched his head. "I guess you are." He looked over the assembled party. Turned to Cocke. Then away from him. "Collins, you're off," he said, momentarily making eye contact with Edmund again. "Sorry, old sport."

Edmund fought with himself the rest of the day. He'd failed to spare Cocke. Godden had won. Repeatedly Edmund jumped to his feet and stomped around his quarters, ready to storm over to Godden and try again to make him drop Cocke from the mission. He rehearsed every possible argument, knowing in advance that Godden would reject it, laughing. There was no option but to go through with the raid. At least this way, he could keep an eye on Godden and watch Cocke's back. It was poor consolation, but it was something.

The next day they assembled in the ops room. Godden had a sheaf of reconnaissance photos. High altitude vertical shots, mainly, but there were a couple of low-level oblique images. Edmund held one up to the light and whistled. You could see the flak bursts. Almost make out the faces of men standing on the field. One of them was aiming a rifle.

"Must've taken big balls to take this one," he said.

Godden grinned. "A friend of mine in the Baltimore squadron. I bet him he couldn't get a useable photo from fifty feet. Cost me a quid, but it was worth every penny."

"I'd say so. When was this taken?"

"Last week."

Haynes grunted. "Anything more recent?"

Godden tutted impatiently. "They aren't going to have moved the bloody hangars, Skip."

"No, but they might have moved the aircraft around. Or the AA defences."

Grumbling, Godden rifled through the prints, and handed one to the CO. “There, that one was yesterday afternoon.”

“Hand me that magnifying glass, would you?” Haynes studied the image. “There’s a lot more fighters there than usual. Look at this.”

They all crowded round the table, taking turns to peer at the photo. It was taken from very high altitude, through slight haze and the type of aircraft was impossible to distinguish, but there were rows and rows of them.

“Maybe there were some squadrons staging through to North Africa.”

“Or maybe the Luftwaffe’s back,” Edmund murmured.

Godden laughed, bitterly. “You and your bloody Luftwaffe. You’re getting a fixation, Clyde old fellow."

Haynes peered at the picture for another moment. “Okay,” he said eventually. “There’s nothing from Intel to suggest any German units but it would be good to have confirmation. Godden, do you know if there’s another recce flight today?”

“Cloud over the target at the moment. Anyway, if we keep sending kites over, they’ll know something’s up.”

Edmund scratched his head. “Look at the way they’re lined up. Wingtip-to-wingtip, twelve to a row. It’s remarkable. They must be damned certain we’re not going to attack. Either that or those are dummies and it’s bait for a flak trap.”

The room went a bit quiet at that. Even Godden lost a little of his sangfroid.

“If it is a flak trap, we’ll be too low and in too fast for it to get going.”

“I’d suggest,” Edmund said, tossing the photo back down on the table, “crossing the coast to the east of Gela town, cutting along the foot of the mountains, then swinging west. Approaching on...” He checked the map. “A track of zero-eight-zero.”

Godden peered over his shoulder and made a sound in his throat. "That won't give us much time to line up."

"No, but it can be done. The hangars are all on a line on this perimeter, running nor' nor' west. Look at the way those kites are lined up. Directly in a row, and the hangars right behind! Strafe 'em on the run in and either bomb them or the hangar."

"If they're still there."

Edmund shrugged. "If they aren't, we just bomb the hangars."

"Alright. That's the plan then." Godden folded his arms. "One more thing. Clyde leads."

Haynes narrowed his eyes. "Clyde? Why? It's your show Godden. Wouldn't he be better as arse-end charlie?"

"It's my show alright, and I say Clyde leads. I'll be arse-end charlie." He sauntered past Edmund, and murmured in his ear, "You'd better hope you were right about this, Clyde old fellow, or I might just shoot you down myself."

The Hurricane was noticeably more sluggish as the three of them took off into the dark with the warlike payload beneath each wing. A good fifteen miles per hour slower. Edmund felt himself leaning forward against the straps as if to will old *Hopeless* on. She was struggling gamely, bless her linen covering, but she was old and worn out. He saw the exhaust glow of the other two fighters in the rear-view mirror. It was comforting. They were struggling on together.

They levelled out at a couple of thousand feet to cross the coast and the first fifteen or twenty miles towards Sicily. After that, they had to get down to zero feet, or as close as they dared in near darkness.

And that was when Edmund realised just what a tough corner Godden had put him in. It was up to him that they stayed low enough that the radar stations on Sicily were blind to their approach. But not so low that they flew into the sea... The course had to be absolutely precise. He was navigating by watch and compass and turn-and-bank indicator. One slight slip would blow the entire mission. And it would be his fault.

The eastern sky had just the faintest glow above the horizon. The tips of the waves reflected the odd watery gleam. Edmund ignored his juddering heart and pressed on. Height around eighty feet. Checked the time in the dim cockpit light, tapped the compass. The coast would be coming up in a couple of minutes.

There! A darker darkness against the sky, and a streak of grey surf at its base. Edmund let the Hurricane rise, just drifting upwards, and levelling out when he thought they would just clear the ground. He checked the watch with its second hand ticktickticking around the face and immediately initiated a standard rate turn onto the next bearing, fixing his eyes on the turn-and-bank as long as he needed, resisting the dreadful urge to look outside and confirm he wasn't about to fly into the ground, or a house, or another aeroplane...

Bearing fixed. Now they should be skimming along the ground in the shadows of the mountains. Wherever the hell the ground was in this gloom... but there was still the odd cue, something lighter to show the Hurri was still at less than a hundred feet. He'd studied the photos, the maps, this was flat terrain. Stick to the plan and there'd be no chance of colliding with anything. The two gleams of exhaust were still behind. Good.

Outside was still almost black. Edmund trembled with the frequency of a violin string. The watch was ticking down. They were above enemy territory. Barely above it. Time. Edmund felt his hands initiate the turn to port, almost independently of thought, curving steadily onto the track that, if all had gone to plan, would lead straight into the hangar like a well-potted billiard ball. The thought made him suddenly aware of the bombs hanging beneath the wings, as if they were dragging the Hurricane down.

The fighter emerged from the shadow of the hills, and immediately Edmund could see better. The sun would just have broken above the ground behind them. With new confidence, he dropped the Hurricane down, down until it felt as though the propeller was almost carving a furrow in the crops in the fields below. There were shapes forming on the horizon. Square, regularly spaced. The hangars! Edmund came up by ten feet, twenty... And yes! The rows of aeroplanes, black in the dawn against the pale ground were still there, lined up as precisely, as illogically as toy soldiers.

He had time to think *this is when we find out if it's a flak trap*, and pressed the gun button. Red tracers speared out from the wings, converging ahead, and flash! flash! flash! pattered all over the fighters just sitting there and he wasn't aware of any flak but he was past the row of aircraft and the hangar was ahead, open, yawning mouth and the Hurricane settled on the air at no more than thirty feet. The hangar was rushing up and Edmund pressed the bomb release, snapped the fighter smartly into a starboard bank, pulled back on the stick and felt his innards drag towards his backside as the G pressed down. There was no time to look back but *f-toom! f-toom!* and the bombs had gone off! He hoped to God they hit something. There's the flak, oh goodness here it is. The lazy lights arced out from guns all over the field. Metal rain.

He almost felt the other bombs going off rather than heard them. Now was when they were to break for the sea, staying loosely together until they could form up properly.

That was the plan.

Unbelievably, he heard the headphones hiss. They were supposed to be on radio silence – though by now the enemy knew where they were well enough. Godden. "Hello Exile

Flight, Exile Flight, go round again. There are plenty more kites to shoot up."

Damn him! But there was no time to argue. One more run. Edmund kept the Hurri as low as he dared, wingtip all but scraping the ground, so low the flak gunners had to be careful about hitting their own planes, buildings, each other, but still the incandescent sparks were flying past the cockpit. He was perpendicular to the rows of aircraft this time, but that didn't matter. He could pepper each column in turn, hop over them and keep on going, straight to the sea and Malta and...

Once again his tracers darted out, playing over the dark flanks of the parked aeroplanes, which flared and bloomed...

And then, the worst thing in the world.

"Bandits, seven o'clock, break left, Clyde, break left!"

Edmund hauled the Hurricane into another turn, hearing the structure creak as the joints loaded up. Another volley of gunfire trails stitched by him, coming from above this time. He glanced up as he held the turn, and the *schwarm* of four Messerschmitts – of course they were Messerschmitts – in a shallow dive, flashed in the sun, lights along the wings and nose twinkling, as more tracers slashed past. They were coming down fast, but he was turning under them. Keep the nose down, throttle through the gate and he could put enough distance to...

"He's on me!" Damn it. Cocke's voice. Edmund strained to look over his shoulder. The *schwarm* had broken into two *rotten*, one of them chasing after Cocke and Godden. Godden was ahead and had a bit of breathing space. Edmund watched as he put his nose down, and kept going, away, away...

"Keep turning," Edmund shouted. "I'm on my way."

He rolled to port and lined up on the chasing Messerschmitts. They had followed Cocke into the turn the idiots. A 109 could never turn with a Hurri. They were trying though, flaps down, full power. In a few seconds, Cocke was out of frame of their guns. He just had to hold his nerve. But if the other two Messers had any sense they would-

A huge crash resounded through Edmund's aircraft, something flashed, and he was momentarily aware of two shapes whipping overhead. God alive. "Reverse," he croaked through the G, then rolled the Hurricane to the right. Cocke reversed the turn, putting him briefly in the sights of the two chasing Messerschmitts, but as they turned to follow, they were in Edmund's sights for a glorious couple of seconds. He saw the flashes around the tail of the aft aircraft before it broke away.

"Viv, they're off you, get out of there!" he shouted. Edmund was weaving, eyes skittering over the instruments, hands testing the controls, hoping nothing serious had been damaged when he was hit. Everything seemed fine. He filed it away. Right now he had to get away. Where the hell were those Spits!

A flash in his mirror caught his eye. An Me109 had latched onto him, it was firing. He kicked the rudder, skidding the Hurricane, throwing off the pilot's aim for a second or two. The Hurricane crashed again, somewhere in the port wing, reverberating. No good trying to outturn them now, the high pair would just pick him off at their leisure.

An aircraft whipped across his path, landing gear down, and he flinched. Not one of the original quartet. Of course, the undamaged fighters from the airfield would be getting into the air now. It knocked the air out of him. That was that, then. He hoped Cocke had got away.

Another aircraft dove by, and another, and a third turned right across in front of him. Oh, joy! They were Spits!

"This is Ratter leader, Blue Flight, take that pair running for it to the north. The rest of you, help yourselves."

Edmund let out a whoop, put the nose down and did not look back. The wireless was full of savage shouts, cries of victory. It sounded like a massacre. He weaved to the Sicilian coast like a madman, only straightened out when he got out over the sea, but once again, Edmund Clydesdale was lost. He had no idea where he'd crossed the coast. The Hurricane was on a rough course for Malta, but the island was tiny. His palms were suddenly damp. How easy would it be to miss Malta altogether, keep on towards North Africa, until the fuel went.

No sense in radio silence now, not after Godden's stunt. That bastard, running like that! He'd have a few choice words when he got back to Hal Far. If he got back...

"Hello Gondar, this is Exile Leader, broadcasting for fix, requesting vector for Hal Far."

The response was immediate and so loud in his headphones it was painful. Thank goodness for Gondar! "Hello Exile Leader, we have you. Steer zero-nine-two."

"Thank you Gondar, steering zero-nine..."

Wait a minute. That would put him some way west of where he thought he was. And that voice, it wasn't the famously gruff rasp of "Woody" Woodhall at Lascaris. Far too toffee-nosed. With a burst of nausea he remembered the time the decoy control on Sicily had tried to lure them in the wrong direction. Damn, damn and blast. A wave of cold ran through him. That was that, then. He pressed on, along the course most likely to take him back to Malta, and was within perhaps twenty miles of the island when the engine began to sound rough. It seemed not to be giving the power it should. *Maybe I'm getting a bit of the Twitch*, Edmund thought. Then the first fine spray of oil began to mist the windscreen. In half a minute he could see nothing ahead.

The words of Thorndike, the rescue launch commander, echoed in his mind. *If you can't get home, don't try – orbit and broadcast so we can get a fix*. But he was already too low to trust the direction finding would pick him up, and the failing engine wouldn't let him gain height. Damn, damn, damn.

Edmund checked the gauges. Everything was nominal for the time being, but falling into dangerous territory. Oil pressure dropping, coolant temp rising. He needed more height. More height to try to spot the coast, to try to get a fix from Malta. Tentatively, he advanced the throttle and as the speed built up, pitched the nose up. The engine took it for a while, and then the power dropped off, black smoke vomited from the exhausts, oil belched out of the cowling and sprayed onto the windscreen. The nose started to fall through the horizon.

This was it. Hardly high enough to bail out but maybe he could bunt and throw himself out. Edmund began to button up the aircraft. Locked the canopy half open ready to jettison. Unplugged the radio cable. Pulled RPM back to economical cruise. And just like that, the engine picked up and began to run again. The nose rose, and in a moment had cleared the horizon again. Christ! He might make it down after all. But he'd just passed through the window for a safe bailout. The windscreen was plastered with oil. Couldn't see a damn thing ahead. Options? None. Keep Going. Hope.

Something in his peripheral vision caused him to turn to the left. A battered, grey miracle hovered there. *Uncharitable*, with the canopy pulled back. Cocke, waving at him, tapping his headphones. Edmund felt tears in his eyes, let out a broken cry. He plugged the radio back in, and his headphones crackled.

"How are you doing there, Clyde?"

Good Lord it was nice to hear a friendly voice. Edmund fixed his oxygen mask on to transmit.

"Visibility's a bit on the ropey side."

"It's OK, Clyde. Stay on my wing. You're fine. How's the engine? Looks as though it's still running okay."

"You know Viv, I think the oil pressure's getting a touch low."

"You bastard," Cocke laughed. "Alright, we're a little off track for Malta. Just follow me round to starboard."

"Wilco."

Cocke's Hurricane drew a little ahead, banked gently and after a few moments settled onto a new course. "There. Luqa's closest. You're all lined up with the field there. They've cleared the runway and the Prang Wagon's waiting."

"Thanks, Viv."

"Anything else I can do?"

Edmund smiled. If he was going to die, it would be with poetry on his lips. "Give me my scallop-shell of quiet, My staff of faith to walk upon, My gown of glory, hope's true gage, And thus I'll take my pilgrimage."

"'Fraid it'll have to wait 'til we get to Luqa for a scallop-shell of whatnot. That one of yours, is it?"

"Sir Walter Raleigh wrote that. I'd rather have written that than flown through Hitler's legs."

"Ha!" Cocke snorted. "You were bloody well low enough to do that when we shot up Gela."

Edmund chuckled but was beginning to feel hollow.

The coast drifted into sight, a friendly buff extending to either side, and then wrapped around him like arms. He almost sobbed with joy. But the ground looked awfully close, with its criss-crossing walls and jutting rocks. "So, how far?"

"Just a mile. Or two."

"Alright. Thanks, old man. You're a lifesaver." He turned to look directly at Cocke, who gazed back from his own cockpit. Waved, and saluted, as the Italian pilot had done.

The engine was holding up, just, but it must have next to no oil in it by now and it might seize solid in an instant. Well, that was that. If it did, he was a dead man. He listened. It was rough, and the engine note was lower than before. The rpm was falling and increasing the throttle didn't help. The nose was inching higher and higher.

But the airfield boundary flashed beneath. The ground was near. Couldn't see a blasted thing ahead!

Cocke's Hurricane, alongside, had its wheels and flaps down. Edmund hadn't the power and he would be going in wheels-up, but he followed Cocke's lead, did whatever Cocke did. *Uncharitable*'s wheels touched, and a moment later *Hopeless*' belly struck the runway, tipped the nose down, shoving Edmund hard against his harness. The Hurri shrieked along the ground in a cascade of sparks for a moment, swung to the left, and stopped. Edmund shuddered with a primal surge of self-preservation, shaking almost too hard to get the harness off, unplug the radio again. The Prang Wagon, siren wailing, was bouncing towards him. He struggled out of the cockpit, sensing a metallic scent, and then the crackle of fire. Ran a few paces, fell on his knees, then his face, and arms were bearing him up.

***

The raid was a total success. The reconnaissance flight, hurrying over at high altitude now the Luftwaffe was back, photographed two hangars completely destroyed, with not a few aircraft in them, and one damaged. It was impossible to count the number of aircraft destroyed on the ground, or in the air after the Spits had arrived, but it easily ran into double figures. And all for the loss of two, old Hurricanes. Edmund would miss old *Hopeless*. She'd proved anything but.

Two Hurricanes and one pilot. Godden had never returned. He was last seen making a dash away from the action just before the Spitfires arrived. There hadn't been anything wrong with his aircraft. Edmund realised with a shudder that he would have heard the decoy controller giving him a false course, and had flown by Malta, out into the Mediterranean, and finally crashed into the sea. They'd dispatched HSL 107 when it was realised, taking a guess at Godden's final course. Nothing of him was ever found.

Edmund spent a day in Luqa's sick bay, then left for Hal Far. There was little for him to do without an aircraft, though, and Haynes put a request on his behalf up to Macleod to transfer back to 801 Squadron. It came back in the affirmative. A Hudson would be leaving for Gibraltar in a couple of nights.

The day of his departure, another letter arrived. He initially assumed it was another note from Vickery, but the handwriting on the envelope was different. More feminine. And there was a local postmark.

With trembling fingers, he opened the letter. There was a short note inside. It read:

"Edmund,

I know you are leaving soon. Be safe, and if you ever come back to Malta, perhaps think of visiting me. I do not think I will be hard to find.

Liena."

He shook hands enthusiastically with Cocke, whose own transport home would be coming soon, clapped Mike on the shoulder, exchanged a polite word with Haynes and it was time to board.

The Hudson rose from the runway, and almost as the wheels had left the ground, the lights blinked out. Too tempting for night fighters to leave them on. It was almost as if Malta had disappeared altogether, leaving only a faint shadow against the paler gloom.

As the dark form of the island receded within the moon-glittered sea until nothing of it remained, Edmund knew he would return. Whether it was weeks or years, after the final victory, which he was now certain of, whenever that might be.

He might go home first. Even ask Liena's God what his plans for Edmund might be. If it still felt right, return, with a thermos of coffee, and wait at the Kingsgate.

But first he had a war to win.

Author's note

'Bastion', like 'Harpoon' before it, is a work of fiction. It is however based on real events, places, and actions. Edmund, Godden and Cocke are fictional, but with aspects of their characters suggested by real people. Malta was a place where pilots who had failed to fit in elsewhere could be given the freedom to thrive, and Godden's somewhat relaxed attitude to the rules and determination to fight the war on his own terms was inspired by pilots such as Adrian Warburton, though Godden's less favourable traits are pure invention. (Sometimes characters decide to take a direction even the author didn't quite anticipate!) Meanwhile, Cocke's artistic tendencies were informed by Denis Barnham, so vividly portrayed in James Holland's 'Fortress Malta'. Lieutenant Commander Haynes was the real commander of 828 Squadron in 1942, though his portrayal here is fictional.

The activities of the 'ASR Flight' and the mission represented at the culmination of the book was based on reality. The RN Air Squadron Malta operated a small number of Hurricanes for air-sea rescue work, and they were utilised on a few occasions in 1942 to carry out 'hit and run' raids on Sicilian airfields in the hope of tempting Axis fighters into the air where they could be 'bounced' by RAF Spitfires. The RNAS raids are not thought to have been quite as successful as portrayed here – the mission depicted was based more on earlier 'Circus' missions that caught the Axis airfields napping, with a dash of cinematic influence from Mark Hanna's account of staging a mock airfield raid in the film *Empire of the Sun*. (The skip-bombing technique shown so dramatically in the film was real and used in WW2).

HSL 107 was also very real, one of a small handful of RAF launches that carried the weight of the rescue operation for much of the war, doing vital work to recover ditched airmen. Joe Pace ('Patchy') was a real life member of the crew, as was Coxswain Timms. Their exploits in 1940-41 can be read about in the book 'Air Sea Rescue During The Siege Of Malta' by Bill Jackson, a member of the boat's crew who served a little before Edmund's spell on Malta.

Many women like Liena contributed to war work, notably in Air Raid Precautions, despite the initially conservative attitude of the Catholic Church which took time to overcome its disapproval of women stepping out from their traditional roles. For information on this I am indebted to the University of Malta for furnishing a copy of Simon Cusens' thesis 'The role of women in World War II: the case of Malta' which gives an excellent history of Maltese women's war work.

Thorndike is fictional, but his barb about 'The Sea Shall Not Have Them' was stolen by the author from a joke reputed to have been made by Noel Coward. It was too good not to use.

Heartfelt thanks go to JA Ironside for reading and commenting on a draft, and Shell Bromley for suggesting a plot development that transformed the character of the book.

Any interested readers would be very welcome to find me on Twitter – look for @navalairhistory – and Facebook, where my page is www.facebook.com/airandseastories

*

Printed in Great Britain
by Amazon